Holidays at Crescent Cove

. . . .

Also by Shelley Noble

Beach Colors

HOLIDAYS AT CRESCENT COVE

···

Two Novellas

SHELLEY NOBLE

WILLIAM MORROW
An Imprint of HarperCollinsPublishers

Excerpt from *Beach Colors* copyright © 2012 by Shelley Freydont.
Excerpt from *Stargazey Point* copyright © 2013 by Shelley Freydont.

EPub Edition DECEMBER 2012 ISBN: 9780062261977

Print Edition ISBN: 9780062261984

10 9 8 7 6

. . . .

A Crescent Cove
Thanksgiving

Chapter One

· · · · · · · · · ·

"It is appropriate that this week of Thanksgiving we gather to officially open the Crescent Cove Boardwalk Historic District." The mayor gestured to the row of once festive, now slightly derelict buildings that lined each side of the street that led to the point.

"Seamus McGuire, owner and operator of the Crescent Cove carousel, will now officially cut the ribbon." The mayor stepped aside and Seamus, once a tall and robust man, now slightly stooped and thin, hobbled over to the red ribbon that stretched across the entrance of the boardwalk, accompanied by his son Jake.

"Mr. McGuire looks frail," Grace Holcombe said to her friend Margaux Sullivan. "Having to close the carousel down last year took it out of him. Hopefully, being able to reopen will give him a little lift."

"I hope it does. It's hard to see someone you've known all

4 · *Shelley Noble*

your life start to falter." Margaux impulsively slipped her arm around the shorter Grace's shoulders and gave her a quick hug. "And if he does perk up, he'll owe it all to you."

Grace shook her head. "I just filed a few papers and let the system take its course."

Seamus cut the ribbon; a sudden gust of wind cut through the November morning and the ribbons snapped in the air—in a victory dance.

There was a healthy burst of applause and a few hoots and whistles. Seamus handed the scissors back to the mayor. It seemed to Grace that he walked a little taller as he stepped back into the crowd.

"And lastly," the mayor continued. "We owe a debt of gratitude to Grace Holcombe and the Holcombe law office for guiding us through the red tape and being an advocate for the Crescent Cove way of life."

Everyone turned toward Grace, and she blushed and shook her head slightly.

"Speech!" someone cried.

Grace swore it sounded like their friend Bri.

"Speech!" cried another and another.

Grace pushed her finger up the bridge of her nose as if she were still wearing glasses. Though she'd converted to contacts years before, she still made the habitual gesture whenever she felt nervous. An embarrassing tell for a lawyer. Fortunately she was rarely nervous when it came to the law. The rest of her life? That was another story.

"Well?" Brianna Boyce, Grace's other childhood friend, came to stand beside her.

If Margaux made Grace feel short, Bri, the blond ex-model, absolutely made her feel like a midget.

Bri gave Grace a shove. "Your fans await."

Grace shot an anguished look toward Margaux.

She was no help at all. "Just think of us as a gaggle of jurors," she said, and pushed Grace from the other side.

Knowing retreat was impossible, Grace walked toward the mayor, trying to smile. The crowd parted as she passed—like the Red Sea did for Moses—and she actually smiled for real; it was so laughable.

Grace took the microphone. "I appreciate the mayor's words and I was more than happy to do the paperwork on this project, but the real heroes are you. All who participated in last summer's flea market, the funds of which are responsible for the new tarmac and parking lot. The citizens who have helped clean and refurbish and bring the buildings up to code. Those of you who have already signed on for the Spring Restoration. For Seamus McGuire and his desire to reopen the carousel. It takes a village to make progress like this, and it makes me proud to call my self a resident of Crescent Cove."

She shoved the microphone at the mayor as the crowd burst into applause and whistles and scuttled back to Margaux and Bri.

They were both grinning at her.

"Not bad, counselor," Bri said.

"Don't ever do that again," Grace said, looking up at her with her most formidable frown.

Bri smiled. She looked tired but happy. She'd just returned from China with her two new daughters, Mimi and Lily. Lily played on the beach with several other children. Mimi stood close to Bri, the older but the less outgoing of the two. And Grace felt a pang of unexpected loneliness.

"Auntie Grace." That's the way Bri had introduced her to the girls. And it seemed to Grace that auntie was going to be the best she could do. Always a bridesmaid . . . She'd been a bridesmaid at Margaux's marriage to the chief of police, Nick Prescott, last month. Now they were in the process of adopting his six-year-old nephew, Connor.

Grace shook herself. It was just the holiday season, statistically a time for loneliness and depression. She just felt a little . . . She sighed. Single? Unattached? Orphaned?

Several people stopped by to shake hands and say how much they appreciated her fight to reclaim the boardwalk and keep it out of the hands of developers. Grace smiled and thanked them but knew she really hadn't done that much. Filled out the forms, badgered those along the pipeline who dragged their feet. It was mainly tenacity and knowing how to navigate the system. Pretty uncreative stuff. But with good results.

She sighed.

"Anything wrong?" Margaux asked.

"Me?" asked Grace. "No. I think this is great."

"Well, Seamus McGuire certainly thinks so," Bri said. "I don't think we've seen him this energetic in months. And it looks like the ladies of Crescent Cove appreciate it."

"The most eligible bachelor in town and having a ball," Grace said.

"Well, good for him," said Margaux. "Oh Lord, would you look at Nick?"

They all turned toward the adjacent beach where the local chief of police, strong and big and normally deadly serious, was turning in a circle, Connor and Lily swinging by each arm, like a human whirligig.

"With all they've eaten today, there's bound to be disaster ahead. Excuse me." She hurried away.

"I better help her out," Bri said, and hurried after Margaux, Mimi still clinging to her coat and taking four hurried steps to each of Bri's.

Grace stood by herself looking after them until she became aware of Seamus McGuire making his way toward her, grinning and practically dragging his son Jake along.

Seamus had thick gray hair and his skin was crinkled from the sun. It didn't make him look old but as if he was carrying around a great joke he was just waiting to tell. Next to him, Jake looked as Seamus must have looked in his thirties. Tall, wiry, with black hair and eyes that made Grace's heart bump.

Stupid, she told herself, and beamed a fuller smile on Seamus as they approached.

Seamus was an old fashioned lady's man who flirted outrageously with every woman in town regardless of age or marital status. It was all good-natured, and though more than a few widows had tried to snare him, so far he'd never showed an inclination to marry again.

Grace remembered him from her childhood when he ran the carousel, and Bri, Margaux, and Grace would come to the boardwalk to play the arcade, ride the carousel, and stuff themselves with funnel cakes, lemonade, and clam rolls.

Bri always rode the same horse, a grand palomino bedecked in jewels and fringe. Margaux always chose her horse depending on what her favorite color was that day. And Grace, youngest and shortest, would have to wait for Seamus to lift her up onto her noble white steed. Always him, because even then she knew she would be one of the good guys.

Then one day Jake, who worked there after school and summers, was there to lift her onto her horse. The boy she'd hardly ever noticed suddenly looked extremely tall, and not at all the gawky, goofy kid who sometimes sneaked them in to ride for free.

He hoisted her into the saddle and looked up at her, and she felt a little dizzy. She'd just turned eleven, and though she didn't realize it until much later, that would be her first experience of infatuation.

It only lasted a split second, and she forgot about it as soon as the music ground up and the carousel lurched forward. And she hadn't thought about it again until she started working on the historical designation project. She'd spent a lot of time with both McGuires while getting historical status for the carousel, which had been the linchpin of saving the boardwalk. She liked them both.

Seamus had become like a favorite uncle or father. Which was more than she could say for her own father. Probably one of the reasons she was feeling a little out of sorts today.

Her own father had barely spoken to her since she stormed out of his law offices several years ago. There hadn't been a family holiday, celebration, or even dinner since.

Spilled milk, she reminded herself, and smiled at the two men headed in her direction.

Jake had become a friend, but every once in a while she remembered that first moment of childhood awakening. Fortunately, she'd never shared that story with anyone, including her friends.

"How's the prettiest, smartest lady in Crescent Cove?" Seamus asked, and gave her an encompassing hug.

Grace smiled. "You're going to get me in trouble with all the widows in town," she said as he let her go and looked at his son.

Grace stepped back. Did Seamus expect Jake to hug her, too? Of course he did. The minute Jake and Grace were thrown together over the restoration project, Seamus had been making broad and broader hints about the two of them, finding excuses to keep Grace nearby.

It was sweet but a little embarrassing. Okay, a lot embarrassing. Jake was Nick's best friend. Everybody knew him. Liked him.

She liked Jake. She really did. But it wasn't like she couldn't go out and find a guy to date. She could. If she had the time or the inclination.

The restoration project had thrown them together a lot during the last few months. But they were both busy. Grace had her law practice and Jake was refurbishing his father's carousel and had taken on the restoration of the arcade as well as his paying work as a master carpenter and woodworker. They were both busy people. They didn't have time for anything else.

Even so, there was an awkward silence while Seamus smiled at both of them and waited for Jake to say something.

It was long in coming.

"Well," he said. "You did it."

"We all did it," Grace answered.

Seamus threw his head back and looked at heaven.

"Dad," Jake warned.

"If your dear mother—" He said in a faint Irish accent.

"Dad."

Ignoring his son, except for the increased twinkle in his eye, he repeated, this time in an over-the-top accent, "If your dear-r-r mother-r could see—"

"Dad, can you cool it with the blarney? Save it for those who appreciate it." Jake lifted his chin in the direction of the parking lot.

Three ladies stood by a white Volvo, waving furiously. "Yoo hoo, Seamus."

Seamus chuckled. "Must be off. Ta ta." He hurried away.

"Amazing how he lost his stoop since the ribbon cutting," Grace said.

"Yeah," Jake said, looking after his father. "Incorrigible. If he's not careful, one day one of his ladies is going to catch him and not let go."

"And no one will be more surprised than your father," Grace agreed.

"Who's for the diner?" Nick asked, coming up to them. He and Margaux were holding Connor by each hand.

"I am," said Connor.

Nick ruffled his hair. "We know you are, sport."

"Bri took the girls home," Margaux explained. "They were pretty tired. All three of them."

"Lily's teaching me Chinese," Connor volunteered.

"That's cool," Grace said. It was hard to believe that Connor had come to Crescent Cove only a year before, traumatized and hardly speaking.

Shows you what family can do, she thought. And had to fight the desire to burst into tears.

She really needed to get a grip.

"You guys come," Margaux said. "I've been so busy I feel like I haven't talked to you at all."

Grace shrugged. "I seem to have the day off. I'm in."

Jake cast a glance over to the parking lot where Seamus was holding court. Seamus saw Jake and waved him off.

"Guess I'm free, too."

The five of them headed across the bridge through the salt marshes and into town.

Dottie's Diner was filling up fast, but a waitress led them to a booth along the front window. Someone had left a folded newspaper on the table, and as Grace slid into the booth, a headline caught her eye.

She froze halfway in. Stared at the headline. The diner went out of focus. The noise buzzed to nothing. It couldn't be. It. Could. Not. Be. She touched the paper with one finger, inched it around so she could see it better.

"Excuse, me," she managed. She slid out of the seat right into Jake. There was a momentary scuffle as she tried to get away.

"Grace?"

"Sorry. I just remembered. I have to go."

Jake stepped back to let her pass. She stumbled toward the door.

Margaux ran after her and stopped her at the door. "Grace. What is it? Are you okay? Are you sick? Can I do anything?"

"I'm fine, I just have to—I'll talk to you later." Blindly, Grace pushed through the glass doors to the sidewalk.

Chapter Two

· · · · · · · · · ·

JAKE WATCHED OPEN-MOUTHED as Grace fled from the diner. Margaux ran after her but stopped outside on the sidewalk, and they all watched Grace cross the street and stop at the newspaper machine. She fumbled in her purse, pressed coins into the slot, and pulled out a paper, letting the cover bang shut. Then she hurried down the street with the paper folded under her arm.

Margaux came back inside and returned to the table.

"Is it something I did?" Jake asked.

Margaux shook her head. Frowned down at the table and the newspaper, then pulled it toward her and unfolded it.

Jake looked, too. Something Grace had seen in the paper must have set her off. That's the only thing it could be.

Margaux's finger skimmed over the articles and came to rest on a headline. Jake leaned over her shoulder to read.

CAR CHASE LEADS TO DEATH OF YOUNG
MOTHER AND HER UNBORN BABY
*Son of Prominent Hartford Businessman
Arraigned for Manslaughter*

Jake didn't see what that could possibly have to do with Grace.

Margaux straightened up. "You guys stay and eat, I'm just going to go check on her."

"No." Connor's lip quivered.

"It's okay, honey. I'll be back. I promise." She lifted him into a hug and rubbed noses with him. "You just make sure Nick and Jake don't eat all the waffles." She scooted him into the booth, kissed Nick, and patted Jake's shoulder. "It will be fine."

She grabbed her purse and hurried outside.

Jake sat down on the banquette that Grace had just vacated. Nick had pulled the newspaper across the table and was frowning as he read.

"What the hell just happened?" Jake asked. "Oops, sorry Connor. You didn't hear that."

Connor shook his head. "Uncle Nick says worse."

"I bet he does."

"But *you* shouldn't," Nick said, not taking his eyes off the paper. He continued to read, then tossed the paper aside as the waitress came to pour coffee and take their order.

"Well, do you know what it was about?" Jake asked, pulling the paper to his side of the table and trying to figure out what was going on.

"Not sure, but my guess is it's about that car chase." Nick stabbed his finger at the article. "Grace's father's firm appears to be representing this Cavanaugh guy. See. Holcombe, Lacey, Davenport, and Estes."

"Her father is a lawyer; why should this be so surprising?"

Nick opened Connor's menu. Closed his own. "I don't know. I do know that for some reason no one has said, Grace is estranged from her family."

"I kind of figured that from a couple of the things she said while we were working on the restoration campaign."

"That's all I know. Maybe her reaction was because of that."

"Margaux didn't tell you?"

"Nope."

"Do you think Margaux knows?"

"I'm sure she does."

"Have you asked her?"

"No."

Jake put down his menu and frowned at Nick. "I thought there weren't supposed to be secrets between a man and his wife."

"Where did you hear that?"

"I don't know."

"There's a difference between secrets and confidences that have nothing to do with me or our marriage."

Jake guffawed. "For a man who's been married for all of three weeks, you sure act like an expert."

Nick smiled. The kind of smile that showed how happy he was, an expression Jake had never seen on his friend until Margaux came into his life. He felt just a pang of envy.

The waitress brought their food, and Jake moved the newspaper to the seat beside him. But as he cut into his steak and eggs, he couldn't help but ponder Grace's sudden departure.

He didn't get her. He liked her. Hell, she was smart and funny and pretty in a lawyer kind of way. Not over the top gorgeous like Bri or Margaux, but more to Jake's taste, not that he was thinking about getting involved or anything.

Still, with Nick married, Jake felt like time was running out. His father had accused him of becoming an old confirmed bachelor; he knew a couple of guys who even thought he wasn't interested in women at all.

He just never seemed to have the time to look around for someone special, and he wasn't interested in the few women who seemed interested in him.

Nick was taking turns eating and wiping syrup off Connor's hands and face, cutting his pancakes, eating his own eggs, and looking at Jake as if he expected him to say something.

He didn't know what to say. He felt deflated, in a way. He'd been looking forward to breakfast with everyone, especially with Grace. He'd hardly seen her since the petition had been approved, and when he did see her, she always seemed too busy to talk.

Maybe she was behind in her own work because of the time she'd spent on getting the boardwalk historical status. Or maybe he had just been handy for research on the history of the buildings and was no longer needed.

Not that it mattered. They were just friends.

"Are you still worrying about Grace?"

Jake looked up to see Nick watching him.

"No . . . Kind of. It just seems weird. The way she reacted. Running out of here."

"You were looking forward to having breakfast with her, weren't you?"

Nick's concerned expression was slowly changing to one of speculation. You couldn't put much past Nick. At least he couldn't. Maybe because they'd been friends for about thirty of their thirty-eight, soon to be thirty-nine years.

Jake picked up his coffee mug while he thought of something to say that didn't bust him.

"Margaux says you two are perfect for each other."

Jake choked on his coffee. He quickly grabbed a napkin from the dispenser and wiped his mouth. "What the hell? You sound like a girl."

"And you sound like a guy that's just been found out. So . . . is she right?"

"A girly girl."

"Kevin Foster called Emmet Jalowski a girl on the playground the other day and Emmet punched him," said Connor, seriously. "Emmet got sent to the principal's office. And his dad had to come pick him up early."

"Well, I'm not going to punch Jake. Smart guys don't punch other people. We were just fooling around."

Connor bit his lip and frowned.

"Nick's right," Jake said. "No punching. So what exactly did Margaux say?" He pointed a finger at Connor. "And no telling Margaux I asked."

Connor looked at Nick.

"It's a guy thing. Not a secret."

Jake sighed, tossed his napkin on the table. "Women stuff, kid stuff. It's just too complicated. I never know where I am with either."

"You, from the largest family on the east side of Crescent Cove?"

"You forget I was the youngest. The, um, surprise baby." He saw Connor straighten up. *Please don't let him ask what a surprise baby was.* "Anyway," he hurried on. "They all were socially acclimated by the time they left home. My next sister left home when I was nine. Then there was just me and dad and my mother, and dad pretty much had his hands full taking care of both of us."

"Okay so what you didn't learn about women at home, you made up for in high school. What's the problem?"

"There is no problem. Could we just forget it?"

"Sure, whatever you say."

"And don't tell Margaux we talked about any of this."

Nick shook his head.

"And Connor, don't you tell either."

Connor glanced at Nick then shook his head solemnly.

Nick grinned. "At least he didn't ask us to pinky swear." He burst out laughing.

Jake threw his napkin at him and reached for the check.

GRACE DIDN'T EVEN sit down when she reached her apartment, but spread the *Hartford Courier* out on her dining table. She stood, hands propping her weight, and read the article in full.

Then she read it again.

> A 24-year-old pregnant woman was killed as she left her doctor's office on Friday around 5:30 P.M.
>
> Beth Curtis was pronounced dead at the scene. Eyewitnesses said that two cars ran a red light at high speeds. The first car slammed into Ms. Curtis, throwing her into the air, as her husband watched . . .

Grace forced herself to skim down the page to the part she saw first and dreaded most.

> The hit and run vehicle is registered to Harrison "Sonny" Cavanaugh, son of a prominent local businessman.
>
> When officers arrived at the Cavanaugh residence, the family attorney, Vincent Holcombe, of the law firm Holcombe, Lacey, Danforth and Estes, was already in attendance.
>
> Cavanaugh was taken into custody and released on $500,000 bail pending arraignment.

There was no mistake. Her father's firm was representing that scumbag again. What was wrong with them? Harrison "Sonny" Cavanaugh was guilty of every crime he'd ever been arraigned for and gotten off. Because he got off every time.

Thanks to Holcombe, Lacey, Danforth and Estes. And the first time because of her.

That case had catapulted Grace from daughter of one of the partners to legal wunderkind in the span of a few days. She, the youngest member of the team, had picked out a loophole, an arcane piece of historical jurisprudence flummery that no one else had thought about. It got the sleaze bag off, when they should have helped put him behind bars.

At least in jail he would not have been available for the joyride and robbery that left a convenience store clerk, a husband and the father of five, dead from gunshot wounds.

They had expected her to be on his defense team again. There was talk about her being leading defense counsel. She'd refused. Her father gave her an ultimatum.

She refused again. And then she quit. She'd grabbed a few things from her desk, left her briefs and law books behind, and walked out the door, her father's words echoing down the hallway behind her.

"You walk out that door, I'll make sure you won't practice in this state again." An empty threat. "I wash my hands of you."

Then the coup de grace. "You're no daughter of mine."

She walked out the door. That was the last time she had spoken to her father or seen him. And that was four years ago.

And now Sonny-boy Cavanaugh was back in court, and her father's firm was defending him again. A man Grace had put back on the streets. A man who had killed and who her father's firm had put back on the streets to kill again.

Chapter Three

. . . .

GRACE HEARD THE knock on the door. She knew it would be Margaux, coming to see why she freaked out. She appreciated the friendship, the loyalty, but she was too angry to talk coherently. She was so angry that she was afraid she might take it out on her friend. And that would be so unfair.

Another knock. "Grace, are you in there?"

Grace stood, indecisive.

"I'm not going away."

Grace felt some of her anger slip away. She was really lucky to have friends who cared.

"Do I have to call Bri to come break this door down?"

Grace felt her mouth pull up into a smile. She knew Margaux would do it. And Bri was completely capable of breaking down her door if she wanted to. The childhood friend whose main activities had been tossing her long blond hair at the boys and never doing anything that might break a nail, the ex-model who never ate and went everywhere by limo had developed some serious survival skills since returning to Crescent Cove.

"Grace-ieee."

Grace opened the door.

Margaux stepped inside and the two women stood looking at each other.

"I guess this is about that guy in the newspaper."

"Harrison 'Sonny' Cavanaugh." Grace turned and stalked back to the table and the newspaper whose pages were crumpled from where she had gripped them. She picked it up and shook it in Margaux's direction.

"What is wrong with these people? He killed a man and he's already out of jail? And he didn't even go to a real jail. One of those white collar golf-course places. Justice isn't just."

She saw Margaux smile.

"What?"

"You remind me of those days when we were kids and dreaming about what we were going to be when we grew up. You were always about justice."

Grace dropped her hand. "That's when I believed in justice for all."

"And you don't now?"

Grace sighed, her rage threatening to turn to tears. "I do. I'm just not sure that it exists."

"I guess we just have to take the bad with the good?" Margaux walked past her and into the small kitchen off the living room. "I'm making coffee," she said, her words muffled as she looked in the freezer for the espresso beans.

"It's not just that." Grace said, watching her pull out the coffeemaker and fill the carafe with filtered water.

Margaux looked up. Stopped what she was doing. "I'm listening."

Grace's throat seized up. She couldn't even bring herself to say it. "My fa—my father." Her mouth twisted; she willed her emotions into submission. Lawyers, especially courtroom lawyers, had to always be in control. Use emotions as persuasion, not a betrayal of weakness. "How could he do it?"

Margaux stepped toward her, her arms open, and Grace walked into a hug.

"God, sometimes I hate him."

Margaux gave her a squeeze. "I know, but maybe he thinks he's doing the right thing. Innocent until proven guilty and all that?"

Grace pulled away. "That's all fine and good. But this guy is guilty, was guilty twice before. Nobody can believe in his innocence. He isn't innocent."

"He deserves a trial, though, right?"

"Sometimes I wonder." Grace pulled away, walked over to the window and looked down onto the street and the row of quaint shops that lined the sidewalk. "I didn't mean that. Everyone deserves a trial. And I know all the arguments for defending an obviously guilty person. Letter of the law. Fair trial. I've heard it all before. My father is a great one for rationalizing, excusing, looking the other way."

Grace turned from the window, nearly knocking a glass vase off the end table. It wobbled but didn't fall. *Like me*, Grace thought.

"I got him off the first time. Me, stupid me. And he went out and killed a man. And was back on the streets in less than four years later to kill again. Three innocent people and one of them wasn't even born yet. A baby. God. How can I live with myself?"

"Grace! Cut it out. You did what you thought was right. You refused to represent him the second time. Hell, you gave up your career with the firm and estranged yourself from your family. You're not the one responsible for what that horrible man did."

"But I'm the one who gave him the opportunity to do it again."

"No, the jury did that. And *they* did it again." Margaux went back into the kitchen and poured coffee, brought out two cups and set them down on the table. Then she scooped up the newspaper and crammed it into her oversized purse.

"Hey," Grace protested, but without much heart for it.

"You're not going to sit here all day rereading this and beating yourself up for things beyond your control."

They drank their coffee. Margaux stood up. "You want to come back to the beach house with me? Jude's coming over and we're going over the menu for Thanksgiving day. You are coming, aren't you?"

Grace shrugged. The Sullivan home had always been the gathering place for friends, family, and people who had no place to go.

"Well, I'm counting on you. Unless . . . Seamus said Jake was going to invite you to their house for Thanksgiving.

They'll eat early because of all the grandchildren, so you can do both. We won't eat until after four."

"Jake is going to ask me to have Thanksgiving with his family? Why?"

Margaux let out an exasperated groan. "Maybe because he enjoys your company. Maybe because he would like to see more of you." She waited. "*See,* as in let's go out sometimes. As in, gee, maybe we have a lot in common and we'd make a really good couple, or at least have some fun."

"The only thing Jake McGuire and I have in common is the boardwalk historic designation and that's a done deal."

"For a lawyer, you can be pretty dumb sometimes. He likes you." Margaux rolled her eyes. "Listen to me, I sound like we're in high school. Check yes if you like Jake McGuire."

Grace chuckled. "You do. And I do like him. He's very nice, but—"

"Do I have to call Bri and plan an intervention?"

Grace shook her head. "Besides, Bri is much too busy with her new family."

"They are awfully cute, aren't they," Margaux said. "But she'd come in a New York minute, especially if she thought it would help get Jake in the door . . . metaphorically speaking."

"If I know our Bri, it would be more than metaphorically."

"Well, yeah. She likes Jake, too. In a totally platonic way. Plus he's helped her with some renovation projects."

"Have you guys been discussing me?"

Margaux shrugged, tried to look innocent. "In a to-tally—"

"If you say 'hypothetical way' I may have to call the cops."

"Speaking of cops, I left them at the diner without a word of explanation."

"Well, you'd better get back to them before Nick puts out an APB on you. But thanks. I'm really glad we're still friends."

"Selkies forever," Margaux said, and held up two fingers, the loyalty oath of their secret club where three young girls spent each summer playing and dreaming, and grew into best friends.

"Selkies forever," Grace echoed. "Now you better get back to the diner before they think I kidnapped you."

"Are you sure you're okay?"

"Yep. I think I'll take out my contacts, take a shower, and try to remember why I became a lawyer. Just kidding. Not about the shower, but I'm fine, really."

When Margaux had gone, Grace washed the cups and put them away. Margaux had taken the paper with her and already the details were becoming a little blurred. Grace knew it wasn't her fault that Sonny Cavanaugh had killed those people. At least her head knew. But her heart hurt when she thought of those victims and the families who would have to go through life without them.

JAKE HAD A good mind to go over to Grace's and see what was what. Margaux had met them when they were leaving the diner. All she had said was that Grace was okay. But he had this idiotic urge to see for himself.

Which was so not him. He didn't do sensitive. Actually,

he was very adept at inept. Nick had kidded him about his randy high school days. It was easy then, there was basketball and football, both were "chick magnets."

Jake chuckled at the absurdity. Here he was almost forty and still unattached. Why? All of their friends were married years ago. Except Nick, and that was because, Jake suspected, he'd been waiting for his soul mate.

But Nick had known all along who his soul mate was, even if she'd been out of reach for a few decades. Jake didn't have a clue. And his dad was beginning to drive him crazy. His father was feeling his age. Having to close down the carousel the year before had taken it out of him. Even though he'd recovered some of his former energy since Grace saved their bacon, Jake was afraid there would be no going back. His dad was failing. He wanted to see his youngest son "settled down with a good wife and a brood of kids."

Well, he'd just have to be content with his other eight kids and his grandchildren and his soon to be great-grandchild. That was a big enough brood for any family. Unfortunately it had been too much for his mother.

So instead of turning right and showing up at Grace's apartment on the flimsiest of excuses, he shoved his hands in his pockets and walked back to the boardwalk to pick up his dad and drive home for an afternoon of television athletics.

But by the time he reached the parking lot, he realized his dad wasn't there, and had probably allowed one or several of his many female admirers to drive him home. The more tenacious ones would invariably still be there. Prolonging the conversation, stretching out their time, asking advice about gardening, even though everything was already mulched over for winter. Or offering to make him dinner, since no one believed a single man could cook. But mainly because they were lonely.

Jake didn't think anyone had ever questioned if Seamus was still a married man. They just assumed he was a widower. And they assumed wrong. Technically.

Jake walked across the tarmac and made sure the carousel and arcade were locked. Then he got in his truck and, driving slowly through the few lingering people, crossed the wooden bridge that spanned the salt marshes and drove . . . back into town.

He parked on the street in front of Grace's apartment building, a nineteenth century warehouse that had been converted into several apartments, each detailed to reflect the period of the architecture. They'd done a good job. He'd been upstairs once recently, when he dropped off some copies of the carousel's original deed and licensing agreement for Grace to use in her petition.

He hadn't stayed. She hadn't asked him to.

So now what? Sit in his truck watching her door like some stalker? He should have thought to bring her something from the diner. Shit. She hadn't eaten, and here he sat empty-handed. He could drive back to the diner and get her a sandwich, but he wasn't sure what she liked.

Grace was a pastry freak. It gave her a softness missing in her thinner, sleeker friends. That brought a smile to Jake's lips. He liked a woman with a little curve to her. A little softness. Call him old fashioned, but he didn't go for hard-muscled, whip-strong women. He'd gone out with a few. They had been exhausting and demanding, all night clubbing, marathon sex with a lettuce chaser.

But Grace. He bet she was good in bed. She was meticulous about everything. Jake opened the truck door and jumped out. He was pitiful. Sitting outside Grace's apartment thinking about sex. Better to get some pastries and go from there.

He decided to walk the two blocks to Cupcakes By Caroline. It would give him time to get his head on straight.

Caroline happily filled a box with a couple of bear claws, a couple of Danishes, some éclairs, and two key-lime-pie cupcakes, and tied the box up with a pink ribbon. It wasn't until Jake was out the door that he realized he'd gone a bit overboard. He wasn't expecting a party. And he wasn't asking her to invite him to share them . . . exactly.

His feet seemed to drag as he walked up the flight of steps to the second floor. Hell, she might not even be there. He should have thought to ask Margaux what Grace's plans were. But that would have been obvious, and he'd taken enough guff and questioning from Nick that morning.

He knocked on her door before he could talk himself out of it.

The door opened. "Did you forget something? I was just—" She looked up, saw him and froze. "Oh, shit."

She was wearing a short silky kimono thing that barely reached her knees, dark wet hair framed her face, and her eyes were magnified by thick black-rimmed glasses.

"I thought you might be hungry," Jake said. He thrust the bakery box at her. "Here."

Chapter Four

· · · · · · · · · ·

MECHANICALLY, GRACE TOOK the box. He couldn't have come ten minutes earlier? Before her shower? An hour later? Once she was put back together again?

Did he have to come when she was half blind and wearing one of Margaux's designs, which would look great on Marlene Dietrich but probably looked like a kid playing dress-up on her. At least she wasn't wearing her ratty flannel pajamas. That would have just cut it.

If this was karma, she supposed it's what she deserved.

"Thanks," she said, the box hovering between them like a cardboard chaperone.

"Well, see ya." Jake turned on his heel, stopped. Turned back. "Do you know you look sexy as hell in that?"

And left her staring after him as he took the stairs two at a time.

Sexy? Had he said sexy? And she'd just stood there like a

dolt? Grace groaned as she finally closed the door and gave it a vicious kick with her bare foot. "Ouch."

She padded over to the table. Pulled the ribbon from the box. There was enough food for a party. Had he planned on staying? And she'd scared him away. Or did he expect she would just eat the whole box of pastries? They did look tempting, especially in her present mood, but she'd never eaten a box of anything . . . well, not since she was a kid and got violently ill on Mallomars. She couldn't help it if she had a sedentary job and bad genes.

It didn't help that her two best friends were gorgeous, sleek, thin, and wouldn't be caught dead in a navy blue suit and two inch heels. But hell, she couldn't hobble back and forth from the defense table to the bench to the jury in four inchers, which is what Bri was always trying to get her to buy. She'd probably fall on her face.

But in two inch heels she was unstoppable. So best just to stay in her comfort zone.

She looked around. Her apartment was just like she'd planned it, unfinished brick wall on one side, oyster shell paint on the others, comfortable, overstuffed furniture. Cozy, friendly, the softer side of the rational lawyer.

And feeling singularly solitary at the moment.

Grace went over to the window and looked out. Jake's truck was just pulling out of a parking place directly below her apartment. So close, she could open the window, jump and land in the bed, and ask him what he meant by sexy. And probably break a leg or two, not to mention revealing more of her body that she cared for anyone to see.

"Grace Holcombe, you've got a self-esteem issue—issues." She snared a bear claw from the box and went to the kitchen to make another cup of coffee.

She stopped after the bear claw just to prove she could. Put the rest of the booty in plastic and sat down on the couch to drive Jake McGuire out of her mind. It only took the image of Sonny Cavanaugh killing that pregnant young woman to do it.

She knew she wasn't really responsible for his felonies. Even if she hadn't gotten him off the first robbery charge, he would have made bail, maybe even pulled community service with no jail time at all. First offense—at least the first one he'd been caught at, anyway. His insistence that he'd fallen in with the wrong crowd, saw the error of his ways, yadda yadda. The excuses, the lack of remorse. It made her sick.

God, she remembered it like it was yesterday. How the hell did a twenty-four-year-old get his hand slapped for getting in with the "wrong "crowd? Other men his age were building a career, starting families, going to war, and he was stealing cars and knocking off convenience stores for the fun of it.

Even if she'd bungled the case and he had been found guilty, he would have been back in a matter of months. He'd killed—twice. And chances are he would keep killing if someone didn't nail his butt to the wall.

How could her father, a man she had wanted to be like her entire childhood, agree to represent a man like Sonny Cavanaugh. Grace had worked her butt off to graduate from law school at the top of her class, not just because she was so zealous about learning everything there was in her fight for justice, but to gain her father's praise. She'd initially even given up her plan to practice small town law for, just to please him.

And where had this all led? He'd kicked her out of the firm and banished her from the family. What kind of man was he really?

And why did she care? It was hard to believe that just this morning she'd been envying Jake and Margaux for their families; even Bri, who was making her own.

It was better not to have family if this was what they demanded. Her father obviously didn't care. Her mother was unhappy about the breach. She'd spent the first two years trying to reconcile them and finally just gave up. Grace suspected that her parents pretty much led separate lives. But hadn't they always? Even before she blew the family apart?

Her father was stubborn and so was she. He took her abdication personally, but she was the one who had paid. But it was worth it. At least she had her integrity, though integrity didn't go far toward paying the rent. He was the one who took money to fast-talk a jury into letting the scumbag go instead of sending him to jail where he belonged.

She knew all of his excuses. "Everyone deserves a fair trial, everyone is innocent until proven guilty, it's an imperfect system, but a just system." Was it? When some poor kid, barely repped by a court-appointed public defender, was sent away for lesser offenses, while Sonny-boy hired the most persuasive lawyers with the most clout in town and walked. That was just?

When had her father sold out to the double standard, loophole riddled LAW and left justice behind?

She clicked on the television and wandered over to her DVD collection, looking for something to watch, to bring back her fire for the bar, her belief in the law, a movie where the bad guy gets what he deserves. Her index finger trailed across the titles, *Erin Brockovich*, *My Cousin Vinny*, lingered on *Inherit the Wind* before moving on. to *12 Angry Men*. She'd had enough anger for one day.

Witness for the Prosecution. No not that one; too close to home. *The Firm*. Definitely not that one. *Legally Blonde*. That was tempting. Leave it to Reese Witherspoon to put the legal system right and do it wearing pink.

But not today; today she wanted . . . Ah, *To Kill a Mockingbird*. Now there was a lawyer who was willing to risk everything for justice, for truth.

She slipped the DVD into the player. Poured another cup of coffee and curled up on the couch to push Jake McGuire and Harrison Cavanaugh from her mind and spend the afternoon with Atticus Finch.

"How was your brunch?" Seamus rolled the *r* as he always did when he was feeling smug or had too much to drink. Today Jake was pretty sure it was smugness. It was the eyebrows that gave him away.

"Fine."

"Ah, and it was that good, was it? So why are you home before midnight?"

"Cut the crap, Dad. It was breakfast and it ended up being just me, Nick, and Connor."

"What? Didn't you mind your manners?"

"Yes. She got upset over some law case."

"And you didn't do anything to make her forget it?"

"Just leave it, Dad."

"I'm just saying."

"You've been pushing me at Grace since she volunteered to help with the designation petition—"

"She's a lovely girl, you do well together. And might I remind you, you're not getting any younger."

Jake clapped both hands to his head in frustration. "I know that. I like her, she might even like me . . . a little. But I'd like to handle this in my own way."

"But you don't, son. I've been watching you all winter and summer long. First it was that schoolteacher up at the Eldon School. Nice girl. Then *pfsst*. No more of her. Then that cutie from the sun and surf store on the boardwalk. I saw her today with a good-looking guy . . . younger than you."

"I'm only thirty-eight."

"Getting close to forty."

"Which is a good reason not to get involved with a twenty-two-year-old."

"Hell, even Nick Prescott got himself a wife."

"Yeah, after two decades of waiting. I don't really plan to wait that long. So stop nagging. You sound like one of those pushy mothers who—" He knew the moment it came out of his mouth it was the wrong thing to say. "Sorry, Dad."

Seamus waved him away. "Suit yourself," he mumbled as he walked away. A minute later Jake heard his bedroom door close and mentally kicked himself. His dad missed his mom more than he let on. All that flirting with the widows was just a mask.

And the worst part of it was that his mother wasn't even dead. Though it might be better if she was. God forgive him for the thought.

Jake grabbed a soda out of the fridge and went out to his woodworking shop to sweat for a few hours of hard labor, stripping the ornate antique French mantel he'd scored at an estate sale.

If restored properly, it would be worth ten times what he paid for it, but it would take an appreciative buyer with deep pockets. It seemed Jake was always in need of money, and he would never look askance at a bit of appreciation.

Which brought his mind right back to Grace Holcombe. And the way she looked in that little robe thing. Had she been that shocked to see him? Embarrassed? Or just annoyed? It was hard to tell with Grace. She played her cards close to her chest. Which made him think of that robe again. And he decided then and there that he was going to stop being an ass and ask the woman on a date.

He'd call her and just ask. Tonight. Or maybe tomorrow, or . . .

EVEN ATTICUS FINCH couldn't keep Grace's mind from curving right back to the court case, which led inevitably to her relationship, or nonrelationship, with her father. Why couldn't he just be like other fathers, some working stiff that put in his time at the office and came home to watch television, instead of the brilliant, and—Grace was beginning to believe—unscrupulous lawyer he'd become.

The tears she'd shed over the movie, she knew were partly for herself and her own family. Atticus had stood up for what he believed, even putting his children at risk, and for the first time she saw him in a new light. A man driven, yes, but was it purely altruistic? She clicked off the television and lay on the couch in the gathering dusk, not moving, but wondering what drove people to do what they did.

Which was a stupid way to spend her day off, and a day that should be a celebration to boot. She went to the kitchen. There was a steak in the freezer, but a celebration for one wasn't exactly what she had in mind.

She picked up her cell, which she now realized she'd turned off for the ceremony and forgotten to turn back on. Seeing that newspaper article had driven everything else out of her head. She turned it on and her message queue filled up.

Several calls; two of them were the same. It was a number she knew—her parent's landline. She deleted it without checking to see if there was a message. Stood clutching the phone as her anger surged again. He hadn't bothered to call in the last three years. Why now? Warning her not to discuss the case? Who would she discuss it with? Who would even think to ask her opinion?

Her part in the whole fiasco was long over. He needn't have bothered. No way was she going to say anything. Not even something detrimental to his case. He could go to hell as far as she was concerned. Whether he won or lost, he was going there anyway.

She scrolled down and deleted his second call.

Which left her only marginally feeling better. She needed something to keep her mind off her father and the scum he was defending.

She knew she could go out to Bri's and share in their steamed eggs and rice.

That made her smile. She wondered how Bri was adapting to a change from baguettes and wine to the simple Chinese fare the girls would eat. She admired her friend. She knew what she wanted, she went after it, persevered through a ridiculous amount of red tape, which Grace knew because she had helped Bri navigate through some of it.

Or Margaux and Nick would welcome her, except they had little enough time for themselves. Which left . . .

She scrolled through her contact list. Found the McGuire house phone number. After all, it was Seamus's desire to reopen the carousel that had started the whole restoration and preservation idea.

If anyone deserved to celebrate, it was the McGuires. She pressed Dial. It rang for a long time and she was about to hang up when Seamus said, "Hello?"

He sounded as if he'd been sleeping. He was always so robust and jocular that it came as a surprise to hear him like this.

"Hi. It's Grace Holcombe."

"Well, hello there, Gracie."

Grace smiled at the phone. It didn't take him long to change into his Mr. Debonair mode. "Great ceremony we had this morning," she extemporized.

"Certainly was," he agreed.

"I thought if you and Jake had no plans for the evening, I'd take you out for a celebration dinner. I should have asked sooner, but I got tied up."

"We'd love to."

"Uh, Seamus. Shouldn't you ask Jake if he's free? Though you and I can go regardless."

"Oh he's free. Out in the shed, working on something or another. I'll make sure he gets cleaned up nice. When should we pick you up?"

"I'll pick *you* up. Both of you. Say six-thirty? I'll make reservations at the Rusty Nail."

"Yes ma'am, but we'll pick *you* up at six-fifteen. Let everybody see that I've got myself a date with the prettiest girl in town."

"See you then." Grace hung up, smiling in spite of herself. She had fought all her life to be taken seriously, especially as a litigation lawyer, not an easy feat for a woman who stood almost five-three if she stretched.

Normally she'd bristle if a man called her a pretty girl. But she didn't mind at all when Seamus did. Because it was as if he treated her like . . . like . . . a daughter. Why couldn't her father be like Seamus McGuire?

Chapter Five

....

"YOU MAKE ME look like an idiot," Jake groused as he pulled his father's Chevy up to Grace's apartment building.

Seamus laughed. "You don't need your old man for that. Now, go to her door like a gentleman." He started getting out of the car.

"Are you coming, too?"

"Nope, I'm getting into the backseat."

Jake gritted his teeth, but he couldn't stay mad. His father had gotten by all his life on his charm, even with his own children. Jake left him to it and climbed the stairs to Grace's apartment.

He stood at the door for a second, wondering what she'd be wearing this time and steeling himself not to say something stupid. He'd inherited a bit of his father's charm, but not when it came to Grace. Maybe because she didn't react the way most women did and it kept him off balance. Hell, they hadn't even been on a date.

The door opened while he was standing there. Jake started, Grace let out a squeak.

"Sorry," he managed.

"I saw your car and was coming down," she explained.

They both smiled awkwardly; Grace locked her door and they went downstairs without speaking.

"I asked you guys out," Grace said as they reached the ground floor. "To celebrate. So no fighting about the check, okay? It's my party."

"You know that's not going to happen. Dad will insist on paying."

"And hand you the bill."

Jake laughed. "You have his number all right."

"So how do we play this?"

"My suggestion is you let me pay." He hesitated. "You can pay the next time."

He waited to see if she would say, *There won't be a next time,* but all she said was. "Sounds like a plan."

He opened the car door and Grace saw his father sitting in back. "Good evening, Seamus," she said, and Jake could hear the underlying laughter in her voice.

She and Seamus kept up a lively flirtation as Jake drove to the restaurant. It would serve his father right if he dropped them off at the door and drove away. But then he would have to take the chance of Seamus making things even more awkward. And besides, no way was he going to miss dinner with Grace, even if he had to put up with his dad's shenanigans.

He was grown man, ran his own business, a fairly lucrative one. He'd been independent for almost two decades, and his father still treated him like a child. He knew it was through love, but it was damn annoying. Not to mention cramping his social life considerably. Every woman Jake even looked at twice became instant fodder for his father's marriage plans.

He just hoped Seamus didn't chase Grace away.

He did drop them off at the door, but only long enough to park the car. He hurried back before Seamus, the Incorrigible, put his foot in it.

The Rusty Nail was a casual restaurant, the decor nautical chic, with friendly wait staff, good food, and a lively bar that catered to the old-timers in the off season. Jake was sure Grace had chosen it because it was one of his father's favorites. How she'd learned that fact was a mystery to him. But it was like Grace to find out.

The hostess led them to a booth where his father helped Grace into one side then sat down in the other, stopping a third of the way in, leaving no room for Jake even if he had intended to sit next to him, which he hadn't.

"Lambs to the slaughter," Grace said under her breath as Jake slipped in beside her. They both laughed, while Seamus beamed beatifically from the other side of the table.

Dinner went well, with Seamus flirting with Grace and joking with Jake. The three of them talked about the carousel and Jake's plans for the arcade renovation.

Seamus reminisced about the old dance hall that sat like a broken ruin at the end of the boardwalk, how it had since been used as a roller rink, then an antique flea market, and several other attempted enterprises that failed to take. They knocked around some ideas about how to bring it up to code and back in style.

This took them through dessert and coffee. After dessert, Seamus sat back with a satisfied sigh. "Imagine all three of you girls home again."

"It is kind of strange," Grace agreed. "I didn't expect Bri or Margaux to ever come back to stay. Just goes to show you."

"Sure does," Seamus agreed. "The three of you used to come over on a summer night all bright with stars in your eyes. We used to call you gals the step sisters."

"The step sisters?" Grace asked. "Did you think we were all from the same family?"

Seamus chuckled, completely amused with himself. "No, it's because you were like steps." He held his hand over his head. "High." Moved it chin level. "Medium." Down to the table. "Low."

It seemed to Jake that Grace's face fell with the hand.

"I get it," she said, with what sounded to him like false laughter. "I was the runt."

"You were the youngest," Jake said.

"You were the petite one," Seamus corrected. "The Mc-Guire men always had a taste for petite women."

Jake shot a fulminating look at his father, who smiled complacently at him. He glanced at Grace, then did a double take. Was she blushing?

"And I have a thing for men who can flirt on a full stomach," she quipped back.

She seemed totally at ease. Jake must have imagined that blush. Probably just the restaurant lighting.

The waitress brought the check, and Seamus quickly snatched it from her hand, then handed it to Jake. Beside him, Grace cut back a laugh and looked at her coffee cup.

Jake nudged her under the table. And they both almost lost it.

Finally the bill was paid and they were on their way out of the restaurant. At the entrance to the bar, Seamus stopped.

"There's a couple of buddies of mine." He waved to two locals sitting at the bar and they motioned to him. "I think I'll just stay and chat for a while. Don't worry about me, I'll get a ride home. Thanks for dinner, my dear." He leaned over and kissed Grace's cheek. "Take this boy out dancing or something." He winked and practically jogged into the bar and his friends.

"Not subtle, my dad."

"No, but he's so cute."

Not always, Jake thought. *Not always.*

THEY DIDN'T GO dancing, for which Grace was grateful. She'd worn her four inch heels and they were killing her feet. Even so, the top of her head barely came to Jake's nose. And everytime she glanced over at him as they walked to the car, she was on eye level with his mouth. And she couldn't resist the little thrill that effervesced inside her.

She was a woman, single. Of course she would be attracted to a good-looking man. It didn't mean anything. She was sure he was just being polite. He liked her okay, but she reminded herself not to get any ideas.

The McGuire men might like petite women, but Grace had no illusions about herself. She wasn't petite; she was short. She was not delicate, she was substantial, not fat, but she'd never be considered thin. And as far as she was concerned if you didn't have thin genes like Bri, it was too damn much sacrificing for a size six.

She liked herself. And that was enough for her—most of the time.

Jake parked in front of her building and Grace started to get out.

"I thought maybe we could have a drink at that new bar around the corner," he said. "It's still open. Or is it too late? You have to work in the morning."

"So do you," Grace said.

"Yeah, but since we're both our own bosses, the only people to yell at us if we come in late tomorrow are ourselves."

"Sounds like a plan."

They walked back toward Main Street. It was colder now, and Grace pulled her coat collar up to her ears. And that's when Jake moved closer and put his arm around her. She pretended not to notice, though she had to admit it was nice.

They reached the bar, The Four Hops, much too soon. Inside, it was combination of trendy and woodsy, with a big fireplace burning Duraflame logs. It wasn't crowded; it was off season and late on a Sunday. They stopped long enough to hand their coats to a coat check person, who Grace sincerely hoped was not depending on tips for her living.

Then found seats at a round pub table. Grace put her purse on the table and climbed onto the high stool; Jake pulled his stool around closer, so instead of facing each other, they were shoulder-to-shoulder, more or less.

They ordered drinks and fell into a somewhat awkward silence.

We should have kept walking, Grace thought. She was better on the move, and so obviously was Jake.

The bar maid returned with a cognac for Grace and a Jameson's for Jake.

"I've enjoyed tonight," he said. "But I should apologize for my dad. He sometimes doesn't know when to leave well enough alone. I hope he didn't make you feel uncomfortable."

"Not at all."

"I've been meaning to ask you to dinner, I don't know why I didn't, I'm usually pretty outgoing."

"Could be the part about living in a fishbowl that put you off." Grace took a sip of the cognac, let it warm her down to her stomach.

Jake pushed his glass back and forth beneath his fingers. "I do feel like everyone is watching every move."

"With every one of them cheering us on."

"Yeah. Do you mind?"

Grace thought about it. Of course they couldn't just play things by ear, be spontaneous let things go where they might go; not with everyone waiting to see if the relationship would take. It didn't have a chance under those circumstances. "No. It just makes it harder to act normal."

"Yeah."

"So what do you want to do? We can announce that we're just friends, which we are."

"True? But I'm not averse to seeing where things might go."

Grace laughed. "You sound like a lawyer. Why don't we just play it by ear?"

Her purse began to buzz.

Grace just looked at it. Who would be calling her this late on a Sunday night? There could only be one person, the last person she intended to talk to.

"Do you need to answer that? It might be important."

"I doubt it." She reached in her purse and checked caller ID. Her parents' landline. The call went to voice mail He didn't leave a message. She slid the phone back in her purse. "No, nothing important."

"What's wrong? Do you need to take the call? Really, it's okay. I won't be offended."

"Thanks, but I don't. It's my father. He hasn't called me in nearly four years so I think he can wait."

"You . . . don't get along?"

"You could say that."

"And that's what upset you this morning at the diner. The article about the case they're defending."

Grace sighed. "Yeah, sorry about that. It was just such a shock."

"That his firm would be representing that Cavanaugh guy?"

"Didn't Nick tell you?"

"Nick didn't know. Just said the two of you were estranged."

Margaux hadn't told Nick, Grace realized. Margaux knew it was something she didn't want known, and hadn't even told her husband. The true measure of a friend.

She looked at Jake. Was she ready to talk about it? Was Jake the person to tell her side of the story to? Would getting it out in the open finally lay it to rest? And she realized the answer was yes.

"Well, here's what happened . . ."

Strangely enough it only took a few minutes to tell from first meeting Sonny Cavanaugh until the current case. And yet it had colored her whole life for the past four years. "It doesn't sound like much now, but . . ." She shrugged, not knowing how to say it.

"You feel responsible."

"Well, yeah, how did you know?"

"Because I know you."

She gave him an incredulous look.

"I mean you just seem like you always want to do what's right."

Grace smiled, a little sadly. "When Margaux and Bri and I were growing up, we had this secret hideout."

"I know. I've been there."

"You have?"

"Connor showed me. He said it was a place that made wishes come true."

"What a sweetie. It's more like it's where we dreamed of what we would be when we grew up."

"You wanted to save the world from the bad guys."

"How did you guess?"

"You always rode the white horse."

He remembered that? "I was pretty naïve."

"You were cute."

Her phone buzzed again. She growled at it.

Jake stood. "Come on, let's get out of here. And maybe we can outrun that noise."

He helped her on with her coat and guided her out the door, where his arm slipped around her, naturally, like it had never left. They walked back toward her apartment and Grace began to wonder what was going to happen next.

Halfway up the block Jake stopped, turned her around and pulled her up into a kiss.

She had been expecting it and not expecting it, and now that she was here, she relaxed into it, let the kiss pour over her, warming her like the cognac had before.

It ended as quickly as it had begun and as seamlessly, and they were walking down the street toward her apartment. *Her apartment.* Grace took a deep breath.

They had almost reached her building when a man stepped out of the shadows. Jake automatically pushed Grace behind him.

She grabbed at the back of his coat. "Careful."

What was going on? Crescent Cove was a safe town. She peered around Jake's arm and her heart stuttered to a stop, then banged, stuttered, and began to race.

She wasn't afraid, just taken off guard, and incredibly defeated. On top of everything else, he had come to wreck her personal life. She stepped out from behind Jake.

"What are you doing here?"

"I tried to call."

Yeah, but it must have been her mother calling a few minutes before. He would never been able to make it to Crescent Cove from Hartford in that time. She should have answered the phone like Jake had suggested. Her mother must have been trying to warn her. So why hadn't she left a message? Because she probably guessed that Grace would erase it without listening.

Damn and double damn.

"I don't know why you're here, to ask advice or to humiliate me. But I'm not interested in either, so you can turn around and go home. I'll phone mother and tell her you're on your way—so she won't worry."

"Grace—"

"Go." Grace practically ran past him. She was too enraged and heartsick to manage more. And she couldn't imagine what Jake must be thinking. He would probably despise her, too. Well, to hell with them all.

At this point Grace didn't even care. She just wanted to be alone, to drown her sorrows in tears, maybe a few muffled screams into her pillow. Leave it to dear old dad to find the perfect time to screw up her life.

She began fumbling for her keys before she even reached her door. She could only think about escape.

But Jake followed her up the stairs; he eased the keys from her fingers and opened her door.

"Sorry about that. Thanks for—"

He pushed her inside and shut the door.

"Jake, I'm sorry, but could you just go?"

"I will, but not until I know you're going to be all right."

"I'm—I'm— How dare he come here?" She spun away from him and began to pace. She knew she should cool it. He probably thought she was a nutcase. But she'd been holding this all in for years and she was finished letting it rule her life. Starting now. "What does he want from me?"

Jake stepped toward her, took both her shoulders. You could ask him."

"I wouldn't give him the satisfaction. I'm sorry he ruined the evening. And I had such a nice time."

He pulled her close. "He only ruined the last few minutes, and what might have happened later . . . who knows? Are you going to be all right?"

"Yes, I really am sorry, Jake."

"Don't be." He lifted her chin. Kissed her, this time longer and harder, and she let her emotion flow out into that kiss. They were both breathless when she pulled away.

"Good night. Gracie."

He made her smile and that hurt even more.

She followed him to the door. She didn't even think about asking him to stay.

"Lock your door. Call me if you need . . . anything. I mean it."

"Thanks."

He waited until she closed and locked the door, then she listened to his steps on the stairs until they echoed away.

She leaned her head against the door. Angry and hurt

and turned on, and feeling like she'd missed another chance for happiness. Which was ridiculous; it had been dinner and a kiss. She tried to hold onto the memory of that kiss, but the image of her father standing in the shadows shattered it.

She hoped like hell he wasn't waiting to waylay Jake or that he'd wait until Jake was gone and creep up the stairs like the devious creature he was.

Her phone buzzed and Grace gave it up. "Hi, Mom."

"Grace, your father hasn't come home. I'm worried sick. He—"

"Don't be. He's in Crescent Cove. I assume he'll be driving back to Hartford tonight."

"What's he doing there? Did you talk to him? Did he come to see you?"

"I don't know. We didn't talk. I have nothing to say to him. I suggest you ask him yourself when he gets home."

"If he comes home. He isn't answering his cell. He evidently hasn't been to the office in several days. Where has he been going when he leaves the house?" Her mother's voice climbed the scale. "They have some big case starting in a few days and the partners are worried and angry. He's the linchpin of their defense."

"Mom, I love you, but I don't want to hear about any of this. He's fine. He's probably on his way home. He should be there in an hour. And life goes on. And another murderer will go free."

"Grace, you're not being fair."

"That's a matter of perspective. I have to go. Good night."

She hung up. Her father was a brilliant lawyer. But Grace didn't care about brilliance. She cared about the truth.

Suddenly uneasy, she hurried to the window, carefully pulled the drapes aside and peered down into the street.

The street was empty. They had both gone.

Chapter Six

· · · · · · · · · ·

VINCENT HOLCOMBE WAS still downstairs when Jake came out of the building, and Jake didn't know whether to ignore him or go back upstairs until he left. The second option was definitely the best, but he didn't want any potential relationship with Grace to be tied up with the anger that was swirling around tonight.

Grace's mainly. Holcombe looked tired, sort of the way his own dad looked when they had to close the carousel. And even though his dad sometimes irritated the hell out of him, he couldn't imagine being estranged from him or any of his family. Not when they had a choice.

He'd wanted to tell Grace that, but he knew she didn't want to hear anything rational. Her father had basically rejected her, banished her like some Shakespearean king, but it looked to Jake like Holcombe was paying the most for it now.

"Hey," Holcombe called out.

Jake knew he should keep walking. Get in the truck and leave Grace and her father to work it out for themselves. But there was something plaintive in that one word. He turned back to the man. He was medium height, thickset. And there was a kind of charisma that emanated from him, even tired, that told Jake he could probably sway a jury with little effort.

Holcombe moved toward him. "You're a friend of my daughter's."

"Yes."

"A good friend?"

"I think so."

"Her boyfriend?"

"Her friend. The rest I don't think is any of your business."

"It's my business to see that Grace doesn't make any bad decisions."

"No it isn't. You gave up that right when you gave up Grace."

"Listen. I don't know what she's told you—"

Jake started walking again. He wasn't about to listen to Vince Holcombe trash-talk Grace.

"Let me buy you a drink."

Jake hesitated. What did the man want?

"I have to drive home and so do you."

"I—I just want to hear how Gracie's doing."

Gracie? *Damn, he's suckering me,* Jake thought. "Fine, but we'll go to the diner for a coffee, and under one condition."

Holcombe's eyes narrowed. "And what would that be?"

"No bad-mouthing your daughter."

"Is that what she told you about me?"

"She hasn't told me much about you. Only that you kicked her out of your law firm when she refused to represent a man who—"

"I didn't kick her out. I told her she had to choose."

"Which she did."

"But I didn't mean for her to leave."

"People who give ultimatums rarely think that far ahead."

"What's your name?"

"Jake McGuire."

Holcombe stuck out his hand.

Jake reluctantly shook it.

"Fine. Now where can we get that cup of coffee?"

They took Jake's car. The lights were off in Dottie's Diner. All of Main Street was shut up for the night. In the summer there would be people on the street until all hours, but during the winter most places closed early.

"Guess it'll be one of the fast food places out on the highway," Jake said, half hoping Holcombe would decide to go back to get his car and go home.

"That'll do."

Resigned, Jake turned the car toward I-95.

"So what do you do for a living, Jake? You don't mind me calling you Jake?"

Jake shook his head as he tore open a sugar packet and poured sugar into a really bad cup of fast food coffee. "Why don't you get to the point, Mr. Holcombe."

"Vince, please. You work in town?" Holcombe continued, obviously having his own agenda and intending to stick to it.

Jake began to wonder how soon he could get Holcombe back to his car and head him out of town.

"I have a woodworking business, I do restorations and regular repairs."

"Is it lucrative, the woodworking business?"

"Enough for me. Is this some kind of cross-examination?"

"No. I just want to know the kind of friends my daughter has."

"Why?

"I'm her father."

Jake gave up and pushed his coffee away. "With all due respect, sir, you gave up that privilege when you let Grace walk out of your life. It's been what? Four years? And what have you done to repair that rift?"

"I was upset. And she's stubborn."

Jake smiled. She was that. "She is, and she's also smart and caring."

"And she's throwing it all away—"

"Stop right there. Grace is a respected member of this community. She has helped people keep their houses when they were threatened with foreclosure. She's spoken for those who don't have access to three-hundred-dollar-an-hour lawyers. This afternoon was the ribbon cutting of the Historic Boardwalk restoration project.

"Grace is responsible for that happening. Grace fought to give my father's carousel historic status, thereby saving the whole boardwalk from becoming high rises."

Vincent Holcombe's eyes rolled, and Jake had a hard time not reaching across the table and punching him out.

"It might not be as newsworthy as getting murderers off on a loophole, but I can tell you it's important to the residents of Crescent Cove and to the businesses that have been slowly dying out as their livelihoods are being replaced by developments that take, but put nothing back into the town. That beach and boardwalk is the only public recreation area we have, and we were all just sitting around while it went to hell and nearly went under the auction block.

"But Grace wouldn't let that happen."

Holcombe blew out air from puffed cheeks. "And I noticed from the sign in her window that she has to sell real estate to make ends meet."

"We all have to do extra jobs to make ends meet. We're a tourist town three months and a few weekends out of the year. The rest of the time we make do. I teach art at a special needs school. The local bakery teaches baking classes. We're a community, and Grace is an important part of that community."

"A good way to have people take advantage of her."

"If you think that, you don't know your daughter." Jake chuckled in spite of his raging anger at Grace's father. "You don't know her at all. Now, if you're driving back to Hartford tonight, you'd better get going. I'll drive you back to your car."

They drove back in silence. Jake stopped at the BMW Holcombe pointed out, and Holcombe opened the door.

"Thanks for the coffee," he said.

"You're welcome."

Holcombe gave a short nod and got out.

"Mr. Holcombe."

He leaned back into the car.

"You asked if I was Grace's boyfriend. I'm not, but I intend to be."

Slowly, Holcombe pointed his index finger at Jake. "Then I'll warn you here and now, you'd better not hurt my daughter."

"And that goes for you, from me. Good night, Mr. Holcombe." The door closed, and Jake drove away without looking back.

THE NEXT MORNING, Grace sat at her office desk staring at a pumpkin muffin and coffee from Caroline's. Normally pumpkin was her favorite, but she hadn't slept much the night before, between her racing nerves, the resurgence of the hurt and humiliation that she thought she'd overcome years ago, and the unresolved way the evening with Jake had ended.

Her mother called three more times after their initial conversation, to report that her father hadn't returned home or called; he wasn't answering his cell, and should she start checking the hospitals?

Grace told her to wait another couple of hours. And since she didn't hear from her mother again, she assumed that he'd finally made it back to Hartford in one piece.

Now her eyes were swollen from lack of sleep and a few tears she couldn't help but shed. Her stomach was queasy, also brought on by lack of sleep. She was tempted to put the Closed sign up and curl up on her couch with an old movie and the rest of Jake's box of pastries. But that would be unprofessional. And God knew she was professional.

So she sat studying the briefs for her scheduled court dates. Two speeding tickets, a zoning infraction, and a domestic violence case. Not very exciting, she had to admit, except for the domestic violence case, in which a local woman at her wits' end took a shovel to her drunken husband. It was clearly a case of self-defense, but the husband's lawyer had gotten the jerk to press charges.

Grace was ready for them. She'd questioned neighbors and the local school their children attended. Summoned the woman's employer, who would testify to seeing her bruised and battered on many Monday mornings. She'd given that poor woman her best shot. She'd have to depend on the judge to do the rest.

She'd help save the boardwalk; she had other petitions that she could guide through the rapids of unintelligible legalese. And the town would be better for it. And that made the traffic tickets and zoning cases worth it.

And if the closest her name ever got to the front page was in "What's Happening this Week in Crescent Cove," that was fine with her. It was sometimes hard to explain why her life here was satisfying. Some people—her parents included—thought she had wasted a promising career.

Grace knew she'd done the right thing, in her heart it felt right, but there were days when she doubted she could ever make a real difference.

She pulled off a piece of muffin and ate it, barely conscious of what she was doing. Maybe she'd call Margaux and Bri and schedule a girls' night out. Except Bri was always so busy with Mimi and Lily. They could go to Bri's, bring pizza and wine.

And then she remembered. Thanksgiving was three days away. It would be too busy and bustling to really talk until after the holidays, and she needed time to voice her misgivings about her life, her career, and about Jake McGuire.

It would have to wait.

The street door opened and Grace looked up. The bile rose to her throat. "I thought you went back to Hartford," she blurted out before she could stop herself.

"Decided to stay over in one of the hotels out on the highway."

"I suppose mother knows."

"I called her last night."

Which is why her mother had stopped calling. You think she could have made one more call to warn her what was up.

"Why are you here?"

"I wanted to talk to you."

Grace sighed. Rubbed her forehead. He was between her and the door, and she'd be damned if she'd run from her own office.

"I can't see that we have anything to talk about, so that can only mean you want to talk at me, which is the way it always was. Not happening. And don't even start with the 'after all the money I put out for your education' bit. The publicity I gained the firm in that misbegotten law case has more than made up for it, I'm sure."

"You didn't have to leave." His color was rising. His shoulders tensed.

Ah, dear old dad. Angry and arrogant. Some things never changed.

Grace stood. "Old history. I have a life. I have job I love. People I care about. I suggest you go do yours. See if you can't get that scumbag back on the streets for Thanksgiving. Hell, what's a mother and her baby? Maybe he'll go for a whole family or a school bus of children next. I'll show you out."

Grace stopped, horrified. She didn't make wild statements like that. It was coming down to his theatrics. His manipulations. She pressed her hand to her mouth, afraid she was going to be sick.

Her father swayed, grasped for the edge of the desk.

Dear God, please don't let him be having a heart attack.

But he straightened up, though it looked like it took an effort.

Grace forced herself to meet his eyes. *Just think of him as the opposing attorney.* Not her father, her father who had driven her away.

"I'll show you out."

It was a ridiculous thing to say since the door was less than twenty feet from her desk. And she was pissed at herself for letting him goad her into exaggeration. As she walked to the door she could feel him looking, not at her, but around her office. And she knew what he was thinking. A little storefront law practice that she had to supplement by giving real estate advice.

A failure. He was probably disgusted. Which would be preferable to pity.

She reached the door and realized he hadn't followed her. He pulled a chair over and sat down, facing her desk. "I'll pay for your time."

Grace stared at him. She felt extremely close to tears, which was not an option. She'd learn to steel her emotions long ago, mainly to compensate for her lack of height and for being a woman. And then from letting the horror of what people did to one another get the best of her.

But nothing had prepared her for this.

And there was no rational way to get rid of him. Call the police? Nick would ask him to leave but would think she was crazy. Then he'd tell Margaux, who would tell Bri, and they would be over in a flurry of wine and martinis to hold an intervention. But they were both busy with their families now, they didn't need to be taking time trying to fix their broken friend.

Grace was the one who was alone. And who had a nutcase father sitting at her desk.

"I'm calling Mother." It sounded so childish, but she couldn't think of another option.

He didn't answer, just began pulling papers out of his briefcase, which, in her shock at seeing him, she hadn't noticed he was carrying..

"What are you doing?" Grace rushed back to her desk while the cell phone rang in her hand.

"I need your advice."

She stopped. He what?

"Hello? Hello? Grace is that you?"

Grace looked at her phone, put it to her ear. "He's lost his mind."

That's all her mother needed. "Let me talk to him."

Gladly, she thought, and shoved the phone at her father.

He put it to his ear as he continued to arrange papers on her desk; moved it away as her mother's strident voice squawked from the other end.

"Vince, haven't you come to your senses yet? Come home before you get into more trouble."

Grace had meant to move away,. She didn't want to be privy to whatever was happening in her father's practice or her parents' relationship, but her mother's voice was too loud to ignore.

"You've lost your mind," her mother said.

"No, I think maybe I've come to my senses. Stop worrying."

He handed Grace the phone.

"Grace," her mother said. "You have to talk some sense into him. The partners are frantic, it seems he has some papers they need for a case they're arguing next week and they need to prep for it. Tell him to come home before he gets into more trouble with the firm than he's already in."

"Relax, honey, I know what I'm doing," her father yelled over her mother's arguments.

"I'll kill him," her mother said, and hung up.

Grace closed the call. "She said—"

"That she's going to kill me. I heard."

Chapter Seven

· · · · · · · · · ·

GRACE RUSHED BACK to her desk. "Just put those papers back where they came from. I don't know why you're here. I certainly don't know why you think that I will in any way help you defend that bastard. I'm sure there are plenty of—I believe the term you used was "real lawyers"—in your firm all too willing to sell their souls. So just get up and get out."

The color drained from her father's face, and she saw that his hands trembled. And suddenly she was afraid that she had gone too far and would literally be the death of him.

There was a moment of indecision, while she teetered on the brink of falling from anger into concern. She managed to pull herself back just in time. "Please, leave me alone. I have a life I like. Please don't ruin it."

"Grace, you don't understand."

"So you've told me. Often. And quite frankly if it has anything to do with getting a known murderer off, I don't want to understand. I have plenty to do just helping people who need legal help and—get this—deserve it."

Her father's lips tightened until they almost disappeared. Grace looked away. She wondered if she should call Nick after all, but she would not humiliate her father that way, even though he deserved it.

"The law should be blind."

"No it shouldn't. The law should be just."

Her cell rang. Grace gritted her teeth. Maybe her mother could convince him to leave. It was like being cornered by a dog that you think may be rabid.

It was Jake. She moved away from her father and slipped into the corner cubicle where she consulted with clients in private, as private as a one room office could be.

"Just wanted to see how you were today."

"Well, I'd be fine if I could get my father out of my office. Evidently he stuck around over night."

There was silence at Jake's end.

"Listen, thank you for calling. I really appreciate it and I'd love to talk, but I have this situation."

"Need me to come over?"

She'd love to dump this in his lap, in anybody's lap but her own. "No, but thanks for offering."

"Okay, but just call."

"I will. Thanks."

"Dad and I were wondering if you had plans for Thanksgiving? I figured you'd probably go to Margaux and Nick's."

"They invited me, but I think I'm just going to stay home and catch up on some work." She sounded pathetic. She put on a brighter voice. "Though I'll probably stop by for dessert, just to see everybody."

"Well, we would love for you to come to us. There will be siblings and in-laws and children coming out of the wood-work, but if you don't mind a large and noisy crowd . . . Anyway, you're invited."

"Thanks, I really appreciate it, but—"

She heard a brief scuffle and realized it was coming from the phone.

Seamus's voice replaced Jake's. "You don't have to decide right now. Just come. We're expecting you. Don't bring a thing, just your lovely self. Around one o'clock. Or earlier if you want. Good. See you then."

"You heard the man," Jake continued. "Gotta love his tactics. Don't give them a chance to say no. But if you think you can stand it, I'd like you to come. Think about it."

She hung up and thought how nice it would be to get to know Jake better without all this angst. To actually be wanted. Yes, much better. And maybe she could make it happen. But first things first. She went out to battle her father—once again.

He was gone.

Grace looked around the office, suspecting some kind of trick. She looked in the washroom. Empty. Hell, she even looked in the supply closet. No deranged lawyer hiding any-where. He was really gone, and he'd taken his briefcase.

Well, good riddance.

She was hit with a niggling sense of missed opportunity. There would never be a reconciliation. Their beliefs, their mores, were just too fundamentally different. And that made her sad. She ruthlessly pushed the feeling away and returned to her desk to try to get some work done.

And discovered his final ploy.

He'd left the brief sheets spread across her desk facing her desk chair. The sneaky bastard.

Fine. She'd file them right where they belonged—in the recycling bin. See how he liked that. Though he probably had twenty copies. She started to scoop them up. But she couldn't keep from glancing at them, and her fingers slowed at a manila folder marked *Character Witnesses*. Right.

She couldn't resist. The urge was like pulling at peeling sunburn or picking at a scab until the wound bled. She opened the folder, read the list of community leaders, political and government officials who attested to Sonny Cavanaugh's character.

They portrayed him as a boy—hell, the man was at least twenty-eight, maybe older—who had fallen into the wrong crowd. Wrong crowd? He was their ringleader. A thief. A murderer. He was the scab, an infected canker that poisoned everything and everyone who came in contact with him. Including her father. Including Grace if she had stayed to defend him again.

It was already too late for her father, but not for her.

She slapped the folder shut, carried the pile of papers over to the recycling bin and dumped every sheet in before closing the lid. If she'd had an incinerator, she would have burned the whole batch.

Grace managed to put in a useful day of work, though she

did jump whenever the phone rang or someone opened the door. When she went out for lunch, she made sure no one was waiting for her before she scuttled down the street.

Surely, this time he had given up and really gone home. But a tiny voice asked, *Then why did he leave those case papers?*

But as the day wore on, she pushed him out of her mind, and by the time she left for home, she'd determined to forget the whole incident. Pretend it was a bad dream and now she was awake.

When her mother called that night, Grace told her he was really on his way home. He had to know by now she would never help him get that bastard off.

By Tuesday afternoon Grace's mood had turned from relief and annoyance to an unsettling fear. Her father was still MIA. Her mother was hysterical. Grace tried to convince her not to worry, that it was just a ploy by her father to guilt Grace out, to manipulate her into doing what he wanted.

"You don't understand," her mother wailed, echoing Grace's thoughts. "He's done something bad. I don't know what, but the partners are calling here and they threatened me with collusion if I didn't tell them where he is."

That got Grace's attention. "What exactly did they say?"

"I don't know. Just that he needed to come back. What could he have done that's so bad?"

"I'm sure you misunderstood them. You know how lawyers can get on their high horses and start throwing their weight around."

"Grace, I've been married to your father for almost forty years, I think I know how lawyers act. I know every game, every maneuver, every attempt at coercion. These men are angry." She dropped out of her lawyer's wife demeanor and back into hysteria. "And sounding desperate. What has he done? What if he goes to jail?"

"Jail?"

Okay, her father was stubborn, and he didn't blink about bending the law for a client, but he'd never do anything blatantly illegal, would he? Grace thought about the papers dumped in her recycling bin. And he certainly wouldn't give her the means to incriminate him. Would he?

"You have to find him."

"Me? How am I supposed to find him?"

"He came to you. There had to be a reason . . . Grace? Say something."

"I'm thinking."

"I'm driving down."

"No. You'd better stay and wait in case he does come home. If the partners come looking for him, try to find out what's going on and call me. And call me the minute you hear from him."

God, she didn't need this. Until three days ago she'd been looking forward to the holidays, if not with her family, at least with her extended family of friends. Now, it was two days before Thanksgiving, and instead of making cranberry sauce or yams to take to dinner, she was going to have to scour the area for her father, lawyer on the lam.

She considered calling Nick. It was too early to file a missing person report, but she knew Nick would look unofficially for her.

What the hell had her father done to anger his colleagues?

She knew the answer lay in those recycled files. She could ignore them, refuse to act, not be a party to condemning her father or his law firm. But she wouldn't, couldn't, know until she read them.

Grace glanced at the clock. It was almost midnight. She grabbed her keys, pulled on her hat, coat, and gloves, and took the stairs at a jog.

The weather had turned cold, and she shivered inside her coat as she walked the three blocks to her office. The streets were dark, and for some reason a little spooky, but that was probably her state of mind more than anything else. Crescent Cove was a pretty safe place to live, especially off season.

Still, she was tempted to call Jake and ask him to meet her at the office. He'd said to call him any time. But Grace wasn't sure he meant it, and he did have to work in the morning. Besides, she didn't intend to stay at the office, but pick up the papers and study them in the comfort of her apartment. And hope to hell her mother was just being an alarmist and there was nothing incriminating in them at all. Because for all the disagreements they'd had, she didn't want to be the one who sent her father to jail.

She gathered up the papers, dumped them into a canvas carryall, and lugged them back to her apartment, where she spent the next two hours sorting and organizing. For the first half hour she shuddered every time she read the name of the defendant, but gradually his name became just a name as she delved further into the case, and the case became just another case.

It was an elaborate defense. A lot of research had gone into it, from what Grace could tell. So what was her father expecting? Not for her to come up with a solution. She didn't get why he was here at all. None of it made any sense.

As it got later, the print began to go out of focus. She adjusted the project lamp, blinked, opened a list of witnesses. She ran down the names, checked them against the prosecution list. Two had scratched. Two had been added to the defense.

She had a suspicion of what that meant, a suspicion she wouldn't put a name to.

She reached for the next folder. Why all this paper? It weighed more than a laptop. Did her father really think it was necessary to have the hard copies?

Of course not, dummy. He made the copies to leave with you.

Nothing was making sense. The more she read, the more she realized the defense was convoluted and weak at best. Where was their ace in the hole? Was that what this was about? He wanted Grace to find the missing link, like she had years before. She might find it, though she doubted it. Sonny Harrison was guilty as sin. And she'd be damned before she'd help him get off again. She yawned, propped her cheek on her hand and kept reading.

Yawned again. Her eyes were scratchy, the lids swollen and heavy. Maybe if she just rested for a minute. She lay her head on her arm, and woke up three hours later.

Her back was stiff and her hand was tingling where it had

fallen asleep. She pushed herself out of the chair and went into the kitchen to brew coffee, then took a long, very hot shower.

It was only seven o'clock. She could take another quick look at the files before work, and then she would have done her duty, more than her duty. Hell, she had no duty to this case or to the firm. But she poured a cup and took it back to the table, where she pushed a sheaf of folders away and put her cup down.

Picked up the folder off the top of the to-be-read pile and opened it.

E-mails. A score of them. Interoffice e-mails among the defense attorneys. They were vague and seemingly routine, until Grace began to see the recurrence of certain words and began to read between the lines. Sonny-boy's defense team was preparing to coerce an eyewitness.

She dropped the file back to the table. Winning was everything to these guys. Including her father. Stubborn, yes. She didn't agree with his insistence that "the law is the law for everyone, even the crooks." Still, she would never, never have suspected him capable of this if it wasn't staring her in the face.

And now she had been dragged into the whole sordid mess.

She threw the folder back on the table, her whole world tumbling around her ears. Opened the next folder without thinking and came face-to-face with the color police photos of the dead girl. Dark hair, matted and covering one part of her pale face, her arm flung out and her rounded belly vulnerable, its precious cargo dead.

She closed the folder, pushed it away.

There was no longer a question of walking away from this case. But she wouldn't be working for the defense. Harrison Cavanaugh wouldn't get out of paying the price this time. This time she would fight. And if it meant bringing down her father, then she'd do it.

She picked up the phone.

Chapter Eight

· · · · · · · · ·

TEN MINUTES LATER Grace was walking out the door, armed with the e-mail folder and a photo of her father she'd downloaded from the Internet. She walked the two blocks to the parking lot where she kept her car. Her stomach churned as her mind replayed the image of that poor girl lying broken in the street, her rounded belly, her dark hair, her pale lifeless face. Neither the mother nor the baby had survived.

Grace shook her head, trying to drive the image away. Trying to give herself the courage to do what needed to be done.

She was usually fine with sharing personal stuff with her two best friends. But not this. Bri knew the barest details because she had been here when Grace moved back, hurt and humiliated.

And Grace had told Margaux just this past summer, when Margaux was going through trials of her own. They'd never mentioned it again. But she would now. Today. Ask Nick for his advice. Take the chance of losing her friends forever when they heard what her father was planning to do and what she was planning to do to stop him.

Grace stopped by her office and put up a Closed sign; she wasn't sure how much time this would take. And a spasm of fear shot up her arm. That she would be tainted by the whole sordid case.

But it wasn't just that. Grace had lost her belief in the law for the second time in her life. And she wasn't sure she could ever recover from this final bow.

She turned into the Little Crescent Beach community where she'd spent so many summers. She drove down Salt Marsh Lane toward the beach. Passed the house her family had rented every year until she graduated from high school. They'd spent many happy summers there, with her father—like many of the fathers—coming for the weekend, and taking the train back to their respective cities on Monday morning.

Grace always loved that little house, had good memories of their summers there, and thought that when she came back to Crescent Cove she'd buy it. But now she was content to live in town. She wanted nothing to do with the beach houses.

She noticed a thin ribbon of smoke coming out of the chimney and hoped that whoever was renting it off season was enjoying it. Then she shoved it to the back of her mind, where it belonged.

Margaux was waiting by the back door when Grace

pulled into the gravel parking area behind the Sullivan beach house. She looked concerned. And Grace's first reaction was to pretend that nothing was really that bad. But she couldn't hide those things from her friends. And if she were honest, she didn't want to.

She'd been carrying "stuff" alone for far too long. She gathered her purse and the bag of papers, and got out of the car. And was hit by the tingling chill of salt air. It was so much stronger here than in town, it was hard to believe they were less than a mile away.

And sometimes so far away.

Grace had spent a good ten summers here with Margaux and Bri. She suddenly longed for those days, when life was simple, where everything was before them. But only for a second. She normally loved her life, except the estrangement from her family. But though she'd often wished for a reconciliation with her father, this last episode had finished any chance of that ever happening.

"Grace."

Grace jumped. Margaux was standing right in front of her. She hadn't noticed that she'd stopped walking and was standing in the middle of the gravel like a statue.

"Sorry. Preoccupied."

"I can tell. Come on in. I have coffee. And pumpkin bread. Jude made it. I haven't even had time to finish the shopping for Thursday or put things away, so the place is kind of a mess."

Grace let Margaux lead her to the back door and through the mudroom to the kitchen.

Grace stopped again. "It looks like a hurricane just blew through."

One counter was loaded with brown shopping bags. A bowl of yams sat on the kitchen table, along with a five pound bag of flour and a row of sweet onions. A second, smaller table held pie boxes stacked six high.

"It did," Margaux said. "Nick and Connor made breakfast." She pointed to the stack of dirty dishes in the sink. "We were running a little late this morning. Nick's taking Connor to school but he's coming back. The bags over there are from shopping last night. The fridge is packed. Jude's is packed, and I'm sure Mrs. Prescott's is, too. So bring your appetite Thursday. Mom and Nick's mom are so glad to have everyone together that they just can't stop cooking."

Grace smiled. It was so messy, and human and loving, that she had a hard time breathing.

Margaux took two mugs down from the cabinet and poured coffee. She handed both of them to Grace and bought out two small plates and a loaf of pumpkin bread, which she cut into thick slabs. "Let's take this out to the parlor. We might find a place to sit there."

The parlor was as familiar to Grace as her own apartment. Same furniture that had been there for years. And it was just as mismatched and lovingly used as ever. A stack of Margaux's latest designs covered the top of the old knee-hole desk. A basket of trucks, books, and superheroes had been shoved into a corner. A history book lay facedown on the steamer trunk that did double duty as a coffee table. Next to it, a first grade writing tablet lay open to where Connor had been practicing writing his name. Margaux put the bread and plates down beside it.

"Okay, shoot."

It was as if someone punctured the balloon of her emotions. Grace flopped back on the couch. "I can't believe this is happening."

"I take it more has happened since you saw the newspaper article." Margaux slid a plate with a slice of pumpkin bread toward her. Grace mechanically broke off a piece, sending a waft of heady spices right to her nose.

"I don't even know where to start. After you left, Jake dropped by and brought some pastries. Since I'd missed breakfast."

Margaux didn't say anything, just looked at Grace over her coffee cup from the other side of the trunk where she sat cross-legged in a cabbage rose–covered easy chair.

"It was a nice thing to do. But I was still kind of shell-shocked, so he just handed me the box and left. So later I invited him and Seamus to dinner. It was the least I could do. And it was part celebration for the reopening of the boardwalk."

"Hmmm," Margaux said.

Grace slowed down. "Then we—Jake and I—went for a drink—"

"At last," Margaux said. "Is that what you want to talk to Nick about?"

"No. Of course not. Nothing even— He walked me home, and there on my doorstep was my father."

It took a second for Margaux to process the information, and like a good attorney, Grace waited to let it sink in.

"Wow. What happened?"

"I told him to leave. Jake saw me upstairs."

Margaux raised both eyebrows.

"He saw me in."

"Yeah? And?"

"I thanked him and told him to leave."

Margaux groaned. Shook her head. "Not that I blame you. Not with your dad ready to beat the door down."

"That wouldn't have surprised me at that point."

"He never was one for subtlety," Margaux agreed.

"Then my mother called, hysterical because she couldn't find him. I told her he was on his way home."

"And?"

"He wasn't. He left, but he didn't go home. He showed up at my office yesterday morning. I had to leave the room for a minute, and when I came back he'd put the briefs from the Cavanaugh trial on my desk and disappeared again. And that's what I want to talk to Nick about. I need some advice."

She hesitated, and in the silence they heard the crunch of gravel.

"And speak of the devil . . ." Margaux smiled, an expression Grace envied.

She pushed it aside. She was happy for her friend. Hell, she'd been happy for herself until two days ago.

"You want to talk to him alone?"

"No. I need his police advice, but I need a friend's take on it, too."

A minute later Nick Prescott strode thorough the parlor archway.

"Hey Grace. What's up?" He sat down on the arm of Margaux's chair. Looked from one woman to the other. "Is this an official visit?"

Grace shrugged.

"I'd better get you a cup of coffee," Margaux said, and left the room.

Nick slid into her vacated seat. "Okay, tell me."

Grace told him about being estranged from her father, about the original case, the subsequent case and the latest case against Harrison Cavanaugh. "So after years of not ever speaking to me, my father shows up at my door and . . ." She took a breath and jumped in. " . . . left the briefs of the case with me before disappearing again."

Nick didn't say anything, just looked attentive. In the same way a panther looks attentive before it springs for the kill. Grace was glad she'd done nothing to break the law. And she swore to herself she never would, not even for her father, bastard that he was.

"Which doesn't make any sense," she said as Margaux came back into the room. "He knows I won't help with the case. And from the looks of the brief and knowing how I feel, he shouldn't even want me to see it. It's filled with stalling tactics, and, let's just say, what appears to be an overzealous investigation of the prosecution witnesses' backgrounds— just at a superficial view."

Nick nodded.

"My father isn't stupid. Actually he's a pretty brilliant lawyer. Before he went over to the dark side." She leaned forward, lowered her voice, though there was no one to hear. "Which is why I'm concerned. No good can come from leaving the documents with me.

"And he still hasn't returned home. My mother's beside herself. And I have to admit that even though we don't see eye-to-eye, I'm a little concerned. This is all so out of character." Grace had to fight the urge to get up and pace. But years of discipline kept her in her seat.

Nick slid Connor's tablet over and tore off a piece of paper.

"When and where was the last time you saw him?"

Grace told him. "I don't think anything has happened to him, really. But this is so unlike him. My mother has already called hospitals and the hotel where he stayed night before last. He'd checked out. I don't want him picked up or anything. He hasn't done anything wrong but be a jackass. I thought maybe if you could give Finley and some of the other deputies a heads-up they could give me a call if they see him around town."

Nick asked some specifics—height, current weight—which Grace could only guess at. Thinner than the last time she'd seen him was hardly a helpful answer.

Nick tore off the paper and put down the tablet. "Grace, it's okay. It won't hurt for us to keep an eye out for him, in an unofficial capacity. A silver alert type situation."

"He's only sixty-two."

Nick's eyebrows raised.

"He has gotten a little gray."

"Do you have a photo?"

"Took one off the Internet."

JAKE SHUT DOWN the lathe and pulled off his protective goggles and face mask. He might just make his self-imposed deadline for finishing the Cove Inn's replacement balusters.

He unscrewed the tail stock and released the balustrade, dusted off the sanded particles and lay it in the case with the other finished pieces. The original balustrades had been hand-turned, and though Jake liked to stay as close to the original as possible when he was doing a restoration, he wasn't crazy enough to say no to electricity.

This job would make a handy addition to his dad's household account. A big infusion. Thanks to some drunken wedding party and a bit of horseplay on the stairs that broke off an entire section of banister and rail. They must have been some big guys, because until that night the staircase had survived two hundred years.

It was almost lunchtime. He could probably work straight through and finish up today. But he couldn't get Grace Holcombe out of his mind. For some reason he wanted her to know that he had her back. But knowing Grace, she'd just look at him like he'd lost his mind, thank him politely, then tell him she could take care of herself.

Feisty. Guess she had to be in her profession. Hell, she'd been that way since she was a little kid and would come down to the boardwalk with Bri and Margaux. Feisty and bossy, but she hadn't been so guarded. Maybe lawyers were trained to stay detached. Maybe it was because of what had happened with her father.

Ah, to hell with it. Maybe she'd like to go to lunch.

Jake threw his work gloves on the table, hung up his goggles, and cut the power to the lathe. His rational brain told him to wait until she got this thing worked out with her father. But that had been going on for years, and Jake wasn't getting any younger. Or any more patient. And if Nick, the most hard-assed, my way or the highway best friend a guy ever had, could do it. So could he.

Maybe.

Chapter Nine

· · · · · · · · · ·

GRACE DIDN'T DRIVE straight back to town, but meandered through the narrow streets where they'd played as kids. She slowed as she passed the rambling beach house where Bri's family came each year. Parked at the curve in Salt Marsh Lane and sat on the steps that led down to the beach. But even with the sun out and her jacket buttoned up to the neck, it was too cold to stay long.

Besides, she needed to keep busy. She could cruise the streets looking for a lawyer on the lam or she could take another look at those papers and see if they had passed the boundaries of legal. And if they had, would she turn her father in?

Grace parked in front of her office but didn't go in. Once she did, she would be committed to the road she'd have to take, so she sat, eyes closed, her head resting against the seat, trying not to think.

Someone banged on her window and she jumped. Turned to come nose-to-nose with Jake McGuire, who was peering at her through the glass, scowling like there was no tomorrow.

She'd never been happier to see him. She cranked down the window. "Hi."

"Is there a reason you're sleeping in your car?"

"Just procrastinating. What are you doing here?"

"I came to see if you were free for lunch. Breakfast?

Reprieved. "Sure. Hop in."

Jake opened her car door. "I'll drive. You look like you could use some TLC."

He'd brought his truck, and as Grace clambered into the cab, she was thankful she'd dressed in slacks and sweater that morning. Jake closed the door after her and ran around to the driver's side.

He was grinning when he got inside.

"I hope you're not about to make a comment on short people or wide butts."

"I like short people, and if you think your butt's wide, you've been hanging around Bri and Margaux too long."

"All my life," Grace said with a twisted smile.

"Your butt's great. They don't give you shit about it, do they?"

"No. It's just one of my insecurities. So let's just stop talking about it."

"Okay." He was trying not to smile but lost the battle.

It made her laugh. "You are so immature."

He started laughing, too, and for the next few minutes they just sat in his truck laughing like a couple of idiots.

Finally, he said. "Where do you want to go? How much time do you have?"

That sobered her up pretty quickly. "Dottie's, I guess. It's close."

"Works for me." Jake started the truck and two minutes later they were walking into the diner.

Dottie was sitting at the cash register, but she jumped up when they walked in. She was tall and skinny, and had been owner, waitress, and hostess of the diner since Grace could remember. She and Margaux and Bri had grown up on milk shakes and fries with Dottie's famous gravy. She still wore a version of the pink uniform she'd always worn but had forsaken her mile-high French twist for a short, layered cut that made her look years younger.

"Well if it isn't two of my favorite people. Where would you like to sit?"

They sat in a free booth that overlooked the street.

Dottie put menus on the table and beamed down at them. "We've got a meat loaf and a baked grouper special. Also a French dip sandwich and a Cobb salad."

Grace didn't know if the fluttering in her stomach was nerves, anxiety, or the fact that she'd had several cups of coffee and no food except for a couple of bites of Margaux's pumpkin bread.

"Can I get you two something to drink?"

Grace swore Dottie winked at her. She hoped Dottie wasn't getting any ideas about her and Jake, because the diner was gossip central. There was nothing weird about two friends having lunch.

Jake was looking at her, and for a moment she panicked. Then realized he was waiting for her to order.

"Coffee?" Dottie prodded.

"No, I'm past my limit already," Grace said. "Just seltzer with lemon, please."

"I'll have coffee," Jake said. "I'm under my limit since I was working on the inn's banister this morning. It doesn't pay to do detail work with coffee jitters."

Dottie left to get their drinks.

"Are you okay?" Jake asked. "You still look a little pole-axed."

"Compliments will get you everywhere."

"I didn't mean—you look great— just like— Oh hell, Grace, you know what I mean."

She nodded. "You're concerned that I might run screaming out of the diner? I'm sorry about the other morning."

"No, it isn't about any of that. I know you're upset about your father. And that was my inept way of saying I care. Okay?"

"Yes. Thank you."

He looked away.

She touched his hand. "I mean it."

Dottie returned with their drinks. Grace snatched her hand away, but it was too late. Dottie was grinning from ear to ear. "Well how about meat loaf for two? It's particularly fine today, if I do say so myself."

Jake looked at Grace.

"Fine."

"Sounds good." Jake handed the menus back to Dottie,

who gave them another doting smile and went away to get their food.

"So tell me about this project you're doing for the inn."

It wasn't until they were finished with lunch and Jake was eating a piece of chocolate cream pie that he said, "Now, do you want to tell me how you're feeling? I'm a good listener."

"I know you are. It's just that lunch was so pleasant, I just didn't want to think about what's going on in my life."

"So what is going on?"

"In a nutshell, my father is a crook. Well maybe not a crook, that remains to be seen. But his firm—well, I told you about that. Not only didn't he leave the night we saw him, he came to the office the next day, and while I was talking to you on the phone he dumped a pile of papers for the Cavanaugh case on my desk and disappeared."

Jake frowned. "Why?"

"Good question. I didn't look at them at first, but later, curiosity got the better of me. I just wanted to see . . . Oh, I don't know what I wanted or expected but—hell, they don't even have a case except for a few sleaze-bag tactics that, even knowing my father, I wouldn't believe he would stoop to."

"What kind of tactics?"

"Let's just say things no reputable lawyer would stoop to. I've racked my brain as to why he would show me this when he knows how I feel. It's like he's wiping my nose in it."

Jake shook his head. "He didn't seem like somebody who would do that."

Grace snorted. "Jake, you saw him for all of ten seconds on a dark street. You have no idea."

Something in his expression set Grace's alarms off. "What? You only saw him for that ten seconds, right? He wasn't still there when you left. I looked out the window and you were both gone."

"Grace. Now just listen, okay."

"You did see him."

"Yes, but hear me out. He waylaid me, said he wanted to go for a drink. No way was I going to go drink with him and have him wreck his car on his way back to Hartford. So I told him I'd have coffee. We went to one of those fast food joints on the highway."

"I can't believe it. How could you?"

"Grace, it was just coffee. The guy looked miserable. I thought maybe I could help."

"That's just great. Did he tell you he was staying over?"

"He may have mentioned it."

"And you didn't tell me?" Grace threw her napkin down. "You can pay for lunch. I have to get back to the office."

She slid out of the booth, wondering how she could have been so wrong about the guy. Her people skills had gone south with her law practice.

Jake threw some bills on the table and caught up to her. They said goodbye to Dottie and walked out of the diner.

Grace refused to get into it with Jake with Dottie watching, which she no doubt would be doing right now. And she wasn't going to tell him what she thought of traitors in the middle of Main Street. She started walking toward her office, buttoning her coat as she went.

"I'll drive you," Jake said, grabbing her elbow.

She calmly eased her arm away, the rest of her in a slow seethe.

"Dammit, Grace, just listen to me for a minute."

She walked faster.

"I just had coffee with the guy. I felt sorry for him. He looked so . . . I don't know, hopeless. I think he knows he made a mistake by giving you that ultimatum years ago. He really cares for you in his stupid parent, clueless way."

Now she turned on him. "*You* don't have a clue. There is a world of difference between my father and Seamus. You don't know how lucky you are."

"I don't understand why you're so upset."

"You went behind my back and talked to my father."

"I didn't go behind your back. You sent me home and he waylaid me on the street. I was just trying to help."

"Well, don't. There's nothing you can do."

"Jesus, Grace, just talk to the guy."

"Thanks, but no thanks." They'd reached her office. She fumbled for her keys, so disappointed and hurt and angry she could hardly see. "Thanks for lunch." She slipped in and tried to close the door.

Jake stepped into the opening. "You know, you're both stubborn. The other night your father asked me if I was your boyfriend. I said no but I was planning on it."

Grace's mouth twisted. A few days ago she would have welcomed that declaration. Now, her father was ruining even this. She lifted her chin. "I guess you've changed your mind."

"No I haven't. I'm ready, but I'm not desperate. So you just give it some thought when you get a chance, and let me know if you're interested. See you around."

And he was striding back down the sidewalk toward Main Street before she could even reply.

She shut the door, leaned against it. How had things gotten so screwed up?

Driving over to Little Crescent Beach this morning, seeing how happy Margaux and Nick were. Seeing her family's old beach cottage made her homesick for a time before all the anger, the words that could never be taken back, the hurt.

She wished she could go back to a summer, any summer, in that little cottage with her mother and father dancing on the patio to the radio while the burgers sat forgotten on the grill and smoke engulfed the backyard.

Smoke. Grace's brain finally caught up to her subconscious. The smoke. There was smoke coming out of the chimney of the old beach cottage. No one ever rented it in winter. And she hadn't heard that anyone was renting it now.

She knew where her father was hiding.

"YOU GAVE HER an ultimatum? Haven't I taught you anything about women? I knew something was wrong when you went straight to your workshop and didn't show your face for half the afternoon."

"I was just trying to help. And I didn't give her an ultimatum . . . exactly. Besides, I'm not so hard up that I have to beg her to like me."

"Yeah, you are." Seamus shoved his hands in his baggy

trouser pockets, jiggled the change. Rocked forward on his toes, looking like an oversized, menacing leprechaun.

Jake felt the familiar burn of embarrassment. Even his father thought he was incapable of finding love. "I told her I was willing and to let me know if she came around. That's not an ultimatum." No, it just sounded stupid, and arrogant.

"Stupid and Arrogant," his father said.

Jake threw himself into the old easy chair. "I didn't mean it that way."

"I know you didn't, son. And I blame myself."

"What? What do you have to do with it?"

"Get out of my chair."

Jake stood and his father eased himself down.

"Sit."

Jake pulled a straight-backed chair over and sat facing Seamus. They'd been sitting this way since Jake was big enough to climb up to the seat. Man-to-man talk, his father called it. Sometimes it led to a thrashing; physical, until he got taller than his dad, then verbal. Either way, his dad knew how to mete it out. Most of the time it led to a gruff hug, a head noogie, or a slap on the butt.

Jake settled down to see what it would be this time.

Seamus leaned forward, clasping his hands and resting his forearms on his knees.

Jake guessed he was about to get more good advice. At this point he was more than willing to take it.

"Your poor mother, rest her soul . . ."

"Dad, she isn't dead."

" . . . rest her soul, had a hard life. I loved her with my

whole self, but I kept her pregnant and poor. I wore her plum out with my loving. I broke her down and didn't give her enough in return."

"Dad—"

"You listen to me. She was a fine girl. I bullied her and at first she bullied back. Ah, we had some fine fights and some better makeups—"

"I really don't want to hear about that."

"But finally she just tired out and let me have my way. And I took it and didn't even notice. And that's when I lost her. By the time I figured it out, we'd just gone too far to get back where we belonged. I don't want the same thing happening to you."

Jake slapped his hands to his head. "I did not bully Grace. She's unbulliable."

"Maybe not but you did something worse."

"What?"

"You didn't fight her back."

Jake sprang up and walked away then back again. "First you say don't bully her, then ride me for not fighting. You're not making any sense."

"She likes you. But she's a strong woman. You stepped away when you shoulda stepped forward. I didn't learn that until it was too late—when to put up and when to shut up. So you listen up and don't make the same mistake."

Jake sat. "I'm pretty dense when it comes to relationships."

"No, you just lose interest fast. And that's because you haven't met the one. Until now. That Grace will give you a run for your money. But she's got a big heart and it's hurting now. Now's not the time to bully. Nor is it time to stand down. Now's the time you open up and let her come in."

"I don't suppose it will make any difference if I repeat, I didn't bully her."

"Nope, now go make us a couple of sandwiches, and after dinner you'll drive on over and make a place for her . . ." He jabbed his chest with a bony finger. "Here. But let's eat first. Don't do any good to woo a woman on an empty stomach.

Chapter Ten

·········

GRACE DROVE STRAIGHT to Salt March Lane before she gave herself time to analyze what she was about to do. Or even to think about what she was going to do. She was fighting mad. Not the anger she felt about injustice and prejudice, but just pissed off. And for once she was going to go full barrel, whether it was logical or not. She would give him back anything he'd dished out.

He'd had the final word when he made her choose between her integrity and the letter of the law, between accepting a case she didn't believe in and refusing, between staying or walking away and losing her job and her father. She'd walked away. She was too young and too passionate about her work to see any other choice.

But not now. She'd spent the last four years studying and gaining assurance. It had been a long time coming, and she felt comfortable as a lawyer and as a person.

And then her father left those papers in her office. What did he think, that she would turn a blind eye again? Help him turn a hopeless case around by manipulating the evidence? They already had a jump on her there. The only reason for filing all those ridiculous motions was because they didn't have a case.

Her father had leveled the playing field by any means necessary, ethical or not. But she wouldn't let him skew justice, not this time. She wouldn't let that bastard Cavanaugh see freedom again. This time Grace Holcombe was standing her ground, and if it meant bringing his high profile law office to its knees, or getting her father disbarred—or worse, jailed—she'd do it.

She swallowed, but her mouth was dry. Her throat was tight and it burned, but she couldn't get a drop of saliva to ease the pain.

Could she really do it? To her own father? Even if he were in the wrong. Even if what he was doing was amoral at best, immoral probably. She hesitated. Then pushed ahead.

Instead of stopping at the front of the cottage, she turned onto a side street, making sure she parked out of sight. Not that her father even knew what kind of car she drove. Not since she'd given up her Beemer the week after she packed her bags and moved back to Crescent Cove.

She doubled back, hoping she was wrong and the cottage was rented to a nice family with happy children and she wouldn't have to do this today. She skirted the house and stopped at the garage to peer through the salt-rimed window. The car inside was a late model Lincoln; her father always bought American. Which wasn't a total confirmation. A lot of people drove Lincolns. She considered trying to get into the glove compartment to check the registration, but if it was her father, he would have the car alarmed and she didn't want to take the chance.

Surprise attack, that was where her strength lay.

Grace went back outside, noticed for the first time than the sky had turned gray and the air was wet. Snow was coming. Fall would be over. And where would she be? She couldn't see any way to ever be a part of her family again.

She wouldn't know until she confronted him once and for all.

She went to the kitchen door; which put her between her father and the garage, blocking his escape.

Chastised herself for her hyperbole. Knocked on the door; stepped into the galley kitchen and a host of childhood memories.

"Are you here?" she called, and her voice echoed back at her. What if she were wrong? What if she had trespassed on an unsuspecting family? They might shoot her.

"In here," came a disembodied voice. A voice that she knew. A voice that sounded old and tired, and for a tiny moment Grace felt sorry for him.

She walked slowly but firmly through the kitchen and into the living room that ran the length of the house. The curtains were pulled across the front, and only a side window let in the gray light.

There was a fire going in the Franklin stove, which heated

that end of the room. The rest was chill. The house had not been weatherized.

The long room was cluttered with the same old furniture, enough couches, chairs, and tables to fill two rooms. Many of the pieces had been pushed back against the wall to make room for the wooden drop-leaf table set up near the fire and covered with a mess of paper and a laptop.

Nearby, a wing chair faced the fire, and an ottoman, on which rested two slipper clad feet. It was all Grace could see of the man who sat in the chair, but she knew who it was.

As she stood there, a hand stretched out from one of the high-backed wings and beckoned her forward.

Summoning her. Like he was some godless potentate and she was a lowly servant.

But she swallowed her disgust—never let your emotions get in your way—something she'd learned from the man sitting silently near the fire. She carried her bag of papers to the far side of the table and dumped them unceremoniously on top of the others that were already there.

She dropped the bag to her feet, then braced her hands on the table, facing the man she had once loved with complete devotion. He stared into the fire, not even deigning to acknowledge her.

He'd aged a lot in the last few years. He'd never been tall, but he was thickset and bullish. Now, he seemed to have shrunk inside his clothes. His face had taken on a grayish pallor that even the fire couldn't camouflage. He was so still that he seemed almost dead.

Careful, Grace. Her father was canny like a fox. He was probably sitting there like a bump to make her feel pity for him.

Well, it wouldn't work with this lawyer. She stood there watching him watch the fire, wondering which one of them would break and talk first. Because speaking first was a sign of weakness. They were both stubborn enough to stay like this all day and into the night, just to prove a point.

But she didn't have all night. She had other more important things that needed to be done.

"I brought these back." She turned to leave.

"What did you think?"

It hurt to breathe. Grace wasn't sure she could even form coherent words.

"Why do you care?"

Her father shifted in the chair almost as if he were in pain. "I knew you'd see that article in the newspaper and flip out."

"I didn't flip out. I can be as tough as the next person when it matters."

"And this doesn't matter?" He gestured toward the litter of paper on the table.

"Evidently it matters to Holcombe, Lacey, Danforth and Estes," Grace said. "Who, by the way, you might want to call. They seem to be a bit worried by your absence."

Her father snorted. A little sound, almost perfunctory. "I bet they are. So did you get a chance to look at the case?"

Grace glanced at the papers, avoiding her father's astute eye. "Not really."

His lips curved. "You did. I can tell. That's why you're

so angry. Not just because Harrison Cavanaugh is on trial again, not even that the firm is representing him in that trial. But because you know that we have no case, all that pile of garbage is just that—garbage—evasion, obstruction, manipulation of the facts, and a game plan to destroy witness credibility."

The admission hit Grace right in the solar plexus. What was he doing? How could he use this confession to his benefit? She would not play into his hands, but she didn't recognize this tactic, and it made her wary.

"Why are you telling me all this?"

Her father shrugged, a cast-off gesture. "Thought maybe you could help."

"What? Are you crazy? Help you get Sonny-boy off? Not if you were holding a gun to my head."

Her father looked at her, and she saw a stranger.

Carefully controlling her voice, she said, "Nothing has changed in the last four years. No argument you can make will change my mind. I may have a tiny little nothing practice, but I wouldn't give it up for all the high profile cases in the world, if it meant playing favorites with the law.

"You wasted your time coming here. You might as well get in your car and go back to Hartford. At least mother will be glad to see you."

"Help me find the Achilles' heel of this case."

"Are you listening? I won't help. I have half a mind to report your actions to the bar association." She snapped her carryall from the floor and straightened up to see her father grinning back at her.

Grace took a step back. She didn't know this look. Didn't trust it. Was afraid it was the look of a man pushed against a wall.

"I have a few ideas. I need you to vet them. Grace, I want you to help me unravel this defense."

Grace blinked. For several long minutes she said nothing. Couldn't think. Was sure she was hearing wrong.

"Wh-Why?"

Her father templed his fingers, brought them to his lips, closed his eyes. "We got the call almost immediately after the accident." He coughed a bitter laugh. "Hell, call it what is was, hit and run, Harrison Cavanaugh ran over a young pregnant woman and left the scene. He must have gone straight to his father, because we were notified before he'd even been arraigned."

Her father took a shuddering breath. "It would be one thing if Cavanaugh denied it. I might have been able to rationalize repping him again. I wanted to. His father and I go way back. He called me personally, begged me to help with his defense, this once, and he'd guarantee he'd never let the boy get in trouble again.. I told him I'd look into it. He didn't even try to deny that Harrison was the driver. It was pretty obvious he knew that he was.

"But when the police arrived, Harrison claimed someone had stolen his car."

"The report named several witnesses, two of whom have subsequently backed down," Grace said. "Would you know anything about that?"

Her father sighed. "There were several 'quasiwitnesses,'

two nurses going off duty and another couple of pedestrians, but it was after five. Dark except for a couple of streetlights. Easy to discredit their testimony because of that."

"The paper said there was a car chase. What about the guys in the other car?"

"A bunch of punks, guys with records as long as your arm. They panicked, pulled a U-turn, and one of the nurses got the license number."

"Which the defense will say is inadmissible since it was too dark to see," Grace said wearily. "Same old, same old."

"Except one of them ratted in exchange for not being named in any possible litigation."

"Suspects cop pleas all the time," Grace pointed out. "The prosecution will portray them as a remorseful patsy. The defense will attempt to show that he would lie, cheat, say anything the police wanted them to say. What else have you got?"

"The prosecution's strongest witness is the girl's husband."

"The husband?" Grace sat up. "I thought he was in the parking lot.

"He'd gone ahead to warm up the car for his new family and was on his way back for his wife when Sonny sped right past him and hit his wife. She flew a good ten feet. The husband totally broke down during the interview, raved about killing the driver that killed his wife and baby. " He held up both hands. "A fragile witness."

Grace nodded. She'd seen that memo. "Easy to badger and then dismiss as distraught and unreliable."

"It's all the defense has at this point."

"Which is you," Grace pointed out, trying to stop the sick feeling roiling her stomach.

"Which *was* me."

Grace heard the past tense but it took a second to register. "What do you mean 'was'?"

Her father turned in his chair so that he faced her. "I've left the firm."

Chapter Eleven

. . . .

"You what?"

"I've resigned. Quit. Retired."

"I don't understand." Grace moved around the end of the table, pushed his feet over and sat down on the ottoman.

"I advised we not take the case. I was overruled."

"Because you thought you couldn't win?"

He barked out a bitter laugh. "Of course that's what you'd think. And who could blame you? But no. I quit because I knew that Cavanaugh would be willing to reach deep in his very deep pockets to win his kid's freedom."

"Kid? Kid? I wish everyone would stop calling Harrison Cavanaugh a kid. He's almost thirty. Most people are responsible members of society by that age." She bit her lip. "Or behind bars."

"Where Harrison Cavanaugh should be."

Grace couldn't believe her ears. Something was deadly wrong here.

"You were right about him all along."

Grace hugged herself as the chill of his words settled over her.

"Oh, I went through the motions at first. You know me. Old innocent until proven guilty."

She'd thought she'd known him. And she thought he'd sold out for the prestige and the money.

"I talked to Sonny after his father had put up a half mil for bail. He said someone else had driven his car but he didn't know who. That model Jag can't be hot-wired, so I asked him who had access to it. He named several of his lowlife buddies. Bunch of crap. After all these years in court and dealing with all sorts of clients, I can pretty much tell who's lying. I knew he was. He wasn't even doing much to convince me otherwise. He was so sure of himself. So arrogant. Vicious—"

His voice cracked. "The police reports came in. The girl he hit was on her way back to her car after a sonogram. The baby was a girl. Mother and baby died. The father was half crazy with grief. He IDed Cavanaugh, but in his state, the defense will make mincemeat of him.

"But it was the photos . . . of that young . . . woman. I looked at them. And . . . and . . . she looked a bit like you. And I thought, what if it had been you instead of her? And suddenly I knew I couldn't do it. Not again.

"I'm sixty-two. I'm tired. I worked hard to build my practice, but I lost sight of what was important along the way.

Then I asked myself, 'What if this was my last case? What if I defended Harrison Cavanaugh, walked out of the courtroom and dropped dead?'"

He breathed out a laugh. "I felt like Ebenezer Scrooge and the Ghost of Christmas yet to come. So I wrote my letter of resignation, informed my clients that I was leaving, and here I am."

A shiver of apprehension crawled up Grace's spine. "When was this?"

"Let's see. Last Thursday."

"Did you tell Mother?"

"Not exactly."

"Not exactly? She's worried sick. Don't you think—Oh, crap. I've got to call Nick. I asked him to have his officers look out for you."

"The police?"

"Yes, damn it. I didn't think they would be looking for you to arrest you."

"Arrest me?"

"You took all these files. You've compromised the defense by showing them to me. They're going to do I don't know what to you. No wonder they're frantic to get their hands on you."

Her father waved away her objections with a flick of his hand. "I named you lawyer of counsel before I resigned. Technically you're working on the case."

Grace groaned and reached for her cell.

"I found him," Grace said as soon as Nick answered. "Thanks. Sorry to bother you. Yeah, he's okay. Thanks again."

She turned to her father. "You noticed I didn't say where I found you. Now you'd better call Mother and let her know you're okay before we figure out what to do with this mess."

But her father just sat there.

"Dad, move it."

One side of his mouth crooked. "You haven't called me Dad in a long time."

She looked at him. Really looked at him. And her anger and hurt began to melt away. She was helpless to stop it. And she wasn't sure she wanted to hold onto it any longer. He'd come to her. She didn't begin to know what it meant. But she knew she'd follow it until it was over and hope there would be something good at the end. "Call," she said, and began to unbutton her coat.

Her father reached for his cell, talked for a few seconds. Listened for a few more. Ended with, "Okay, okay, I'll tell her." And hung up.

"She insists on driving down. She's bringing food. And says to tell you to go out and get a turkey." He pushed himself out of the chair. "Oh, and that she loves you."

He moved stiffly toward the table and reached for a folder. "And so do I."

They stood side by side, leaning over the table, hands braced on the edge, father and daughter, studying the files of the defense's case.

"What do you want to do?" Grace asked.

"I don't know that there's much we can do. I guess I didn't know my partners at all. Or have I lost my grip? Does this look like a case to you?"

Grace shook her head. "Looks like a case of desperation to me."

"Exactly." He turned to look at her. "But if you think I would have stayed with this case if I had a better chance of winning, you'd be wrong."

"I don't. I've seen you try a case successfully with less."

Her father sighed. "Yes. But was it the right thing to do?"

"I don't know, Dad. I know you can't practice according to whim. That everyone—even the criminals—are entitled to a fair trial. But I can't do that. And this isn't even fair." She picked up a few papers and let them drop. "It's just machination."

"Yeah. You start out in this world so altruistic, so fired up, and then you win a case, then another, and it becomes so tempting to win. You get seduced by the idea of winning. The lines get blurred, what's important begins to shift. You've made a promise to do best by your client, but one day you wake up and realize you're not working for your client, you're not even working for justice, but for the win. And you know you've gone off the rails. Because that's not what the law is about.

"This case gave me my wake-up call. You figured it out long before your old dad did. I wished I had listened."

Grace had never heard her father speak like this. He never brooked an argument except for the sake of finding the weak spots, never from the heart. But this was different. She was still wary. She'd spent too many years around him to think that he'd changed overnight. And yet . . .

She stopped. "But are you really ready to give it all up. Just because of this?"

His brows knit. "Yes, I think I am. I still work ten, twelve hours a day. It's time I let someone else take over."

"I'm not going back to the firm," she said.

"No. I can see you're happy with what you're doing. The other partners can buy me out. I'm done."

Grace shook her head. "I think you should give this more thought. I mean, what are you going to do, play golf every afternoon?"

"If I want. God knows we have enough money to enjoy my retirement and even leave you a decent inheritance."

Grace held up her hand.

"Don't worry. I'm not planning on kicking off just yet. I may even take your lead, do some volunteer counseling."

"Pro bono work?" Grace stammered.

"Why not?"

"Dad, I'm having a hard time wrapping my head around this."

"I know. I am, too. But it's the right thing to do. Oh hell, Grace. I don't expect you to believe that I'm serious about this. I can be a mean SOB, stubborn, but I like to think I'm an honorable man. And this case pushed me beyond that. There have been others, I'm sure. There are bound to be in this business. I just didn't notice, or I chose not to look too closely.

"It's a fine line we lawyers walk. Trying to balance justice, legalities, and humanity all at once. But this case— Hell, the Cavanaughs have been a thorn in my side since they walked into our offices five years ago. I can't do it. I can't represent the guy. Flimsy defense or no, I'm afraid I might win."

Grace shut her eyes, trying not to think about her part in letting Harrison Cavanaugh go free. "Like I did."

"It wasn't your fault. You were bright. We egged you on. We did our best for him and got him off, then he threw it back in our faces. And we got him off again. But this time he's gone too far."

He reached over and tugged her hair, something he hadn't done since she was ten at least. She turned into him and he wrapped his arms around her. And she fell into this deceptively soft, teddy bear of a man. He could be ruthless, often was, but for some reason she believed him now.

"I'm sorry if I misjudged you," Grace said. "I was just defensive. I wanted your respect, your approval, all my life. But I was afraid you would never forgive me for walking out."

"You've always had it. Well, I was pretty angry for a while. I know how to hold a grudge."

"Yeah you do."

"So do you."

"I learned it from the best."

"Yeah, well. Your mother put me straight—eventually. And after that . . . it took a while to get up the nerve to try to change things."

He kissed the top of her head and eased her away, keeping hold of her shoulders. "Your mother will be here any minute and we still haven't gotten the turkey."

Grace stepped back. "I'll go get the turkey. I think you two should be alone when you tell her that you've resigned."

"Retired."

"Retired. You're on your own."

"Can I tell her that everything is okay between you and me?"

Grace hesitated, picked up her bag. "Yeah, tell her that everything's fine. I'll come by in the morning and take you to breakfast."

"You don't want to come back later for dinner?"

"No, thanks. I have something I need to do. See you tomorrow."

Her father walked her to the front door and watched until she reached her car. She made a U-turn and waved as she drove past the house toward Shore Road.

When she reached the exit from Little Crescent Beach, she stopped, deliberating about what to do next. Get the turkey or call Jake?

Hell, the turkey wasn't going anywhere, but Jake might. He might decide she was too high maintenance and take a hike. But she wouldn't know until she asked.

Besides, she'd just faced her father without losing skin, surely she could face someone who wanted to be her boyfriend. A smile crept onto Grace's face. *Boyfriend.* Did people really call themselves that these days? And was he serious?

There was only one way to find out. Heart clanking, she turned left toward Jake's house.

Chapter Twelve

· · · · · · · · ·

"Not here," Seamus said. "Just missed him. Now if you've got something good to say to him, I'll tell you where he is. If it isn't good, maybe you could wait until after Thanksgiving."

"It's good," Grace said. "At least it's good for me. I hope it's good for him."

Seamus cackled. Raised his eyes to heaven. "Can you believe these two?" He looked back at Grace, trying to compose himself. "That's the kind of thing you say in the intimacy of your—".

"Oh." Grace clapped a hand over her mouth. "I didn't mean—"

"I know what you meant. I swear, for full grown adults, the two of you are the most . . . words fail me. He had to pick up a few last minute things at the store. You coming tomorrow?"

"My parents are here."

"Bring them, too, might as well see what they're getting

into. Now, get out of here before you two pass each other in the night." Seamus heaved a sigh, shook his head and closed the door.

Grace practically ran to her car. She felt giddy and stupid and completely maladroit. And she didn't care.

She had to exert iron control not to speed through town toward the Cove Market and breathed a thankful sigh of relief when she saw Jake's truck parked in the lot next to it.

She grabbed a basket and pushed it into the store, nearly running into a cart filled high with bags and hiding whoever was pushing it.

"Sorry," Grace said. She swerved out of the cart's path and headed down the aisle.

He was standing halfway down the second aisle, frowning at a display of canned cranberry sauce. Grace slowed down, suddenly feeling like a teenager about to face the captain of the football team.

Nervous? A bit. But mainly happy and slightly silly. She'd been a responsible adult for as long as she could remember. Margaux and Bri used to kid her about it when they were still kids. Even though Grace was several years younger, she'd bossed them from the get go.

It had been fun then. When had she stopped having fun or allowed herself to relax and think about starting a relationship? Except for a few false starts, she'd never bothered to cultivate a long-lasting relationship. Her work took up too much time. And work always came first.

Jake was still frowning at the cans when she rolled her cart up next to his and gave it a bump.

He jumped. "Sorry." He started to move his cart aside and saw her. He broke into a smile that told Grace everything she needed to know.

"Everything okay?"

Grace nodded. She didn't trust her voice. If she answered, she might burst into song like a demented Disney character. She pulled herself together. "Yes. My father retired. My mother is on her way, she told me to come buy a turkey."

"Oh," he said, looking disappointed. "I was hoping you'd be able to have Thanksgiving with us."

"Seamus invited all three of us. But I'm not sure you're ready for my parents."

"It's more a question if they can handle us. Two of my brothers and their wives and children and my oldest sister and her brood. The others live too far away. Even so, it'll be a zoo. But a friendly zoo. And the store only has frozen turkeys left, it will never defrost in time."

Grace deliberated. Her reconciliation with her father was still too fresh to know what would be best. But it was also time for her to start thinking about her own happiness.

"Plus I'm betting that your father and mine together will be worth the price of admission."

Grace made a face. "Oh, what the hell." She fished out her cell phone, rang her mother.

"Hi dear, I just got here, I'm so happy you two have made up."

She sounded happy. Grace wondered if he'd hit her with the retirement part yet.

"Did you pick up the turkey?"

"They only have frozen ones," Grace said, "and actually, we've been invited to Thanksgiving dinner by a friend of mine."

"Margaux?"

"Actually, Jake McGuire and his father."

"McGuire," her mother repeated, obviously trying to put a face to the name.

Jake shook his head. "Tell her—"

Her father's voice came loud and clear in the background. "The boyfriend."

Grace blushed.

"Boyfriend? You've got a boyfriend?"

Jack made a face, walked several feet away, trying not to laugh.

Grace gave him a look.

"Mother, they're friends of mine."

"Tell them we'd love to come."

Grace winced. This could turn out to be a disaster. Jake was holding his sides and shaking with silent laughter.

"Fine." She hung up and turned on him. "I can't believe you told my father that you were my boyfriend."

"He said it first."

"We're never going to live that down."

"What else could I say? Certainly not what I was thinking. What I'm thinking now."

Grace felt a rush of heat. "And what would that be?" she asked cautiously.

He turned a smoldering, heated look on her. "Whether I should get jellied or the kind with the berries in it."

Grace laughed. "You are so your father. Get both."

········

A Crescent Cove
Christmas

Chapter One

. . . .

IT WAS SNOWING hard. Brianna Boyce hunched over the steering wheel and squinted through the windshield, trying to keep the car on the road. A road that was quickly disappearing beneath drifts of white. They shouldn't have stayed at the mall so long. It was only a little after five but already it was pitch-black except for the blinding curtain of white.

She glanced at the backseat where her two newly adopted daughters were asleep in their car seats. Ming Li and Li Fan, Mimi and Lily. They'd fallen asleep before Bri had negotiated her new secondhand SUV out of the parking lot.

Bri knew how to shop, but she normally avoided the mall. But today with the weather being so fickle, she'd decided to give the girls a treat. And the trip had never given her so much pleasure. They'd taken in everything, stopped at every window to gaze at the clothes, the appliances, the bath products. At the toy store, they stared open-mouthed at a pink plastic fairy castle, and Bri decided to go back and buy it for their Christmas.

They didn't ask for a thing as Bri pointed out things in her pigeon Chinese. They had no toys like this in the orphanage where they'd spent their young lives until a few weeks ago. They had never heard of Disney. Didn't understand that these things could be bought and taken home. Could be theirs for their very own, not just some fairy-tale land to be visited with their new mother.

They were afraid to sit on Santa's lap, which was a bit of a disappointment. She'd had fantasies of sending out Christmas cards with them smiling, each on one knee. Bri tried to see the mall Santa through their eyes. He was pretty good, a huge man, well padded in his red suit, a white curly beard, and a Santa hat with big white pompom that hung over his forehead.

They'd taken one look and cowered against her. His "Ho ho ho" scared them. Bri smiled, bittersweet. Maybe next year when they were more accustomed to living here.

When Bri had started adoption proceedings, they'd been three and two. Now Mimi was five and Lily almost four. It seemed like eons before she was finally allowed to bring them home at the beginning of November. And Bri was thankful. She had a lot to be thankful about.

She looked back at the road, slowed as she came to the curve a quarter mile from their home, an old horse farm she'd bought when she returned to Crescent Cove eight years before.

The SUV took the turn easily. She would never drive too fast again. She'd learned that lesson many years before.

Up ahead she could see something standing by the side of the road. A deer? She slowed even more. But as the SUV got closer she could see that it was a man, his arm lifted in the air. A hitchhiker. In this weather.

Bri's first thought was to slow down and give the poor man a ride, no one should be out in this weather. She might have done it in her younger years when she was fearless and thought she was invincible. She might even have picked him up a few weeks ago, and taken her chances that he wasn't a psychopath.

But she had someone other than herself to think of now. To protect. So she gave him a wide berth and left him to his lonely, frigid trek toward town.

A quarter of a mile later she turned into her driveway. Drove right up to the side of the old clapboard house and stopped at the kitchen door. Mimi roused as Bri lifted her out of the car, and she sleepily clasped her little arms around Bri's neck. She was light as a feather. Any qualms Bri might have had about taking care of two young girls while being hampered by her gimpy leg had fallen by the wayside the minute she'd given them her first hug.

Some things were a bit dicey, like carrying them through the snow to the house. One of the reasons for parking right at the door. And it was awkward getting up the steps. But nothing she couldn't handle and nothing she begrudged. She couldn't help but give Mimi a little squeeze as they reached the warmth of the kitchen.

She went straight through to the great room, the warmest room in the drafty old house, where they spent most of their time. She deposited Mimi at one end of the funky overstuffed sofa, then went back for Lily.

Lily didn't even rouse as Bri laid her at the opposite end of the couch. She covered them both with the colorful afghan she'd purchased at the town flea market the summer before, and went back outside to collect her mall purchases.

As she beeped the SUV locked, a gust of wind whipped through the air and she shivered as she hurried into the house. She dumped everything on the kitchen table, pulled off her hat and gloves, shrugged out of her coat, and took out her cell. Punched in a number she had on speed dial.

"Hey, Bri. What's up?"

"Hi, Nick, no emergency. Just that I saw a hitchhiker on our way home from the mall."

"You didn't pick him up?" Nick Prescott was the interim sheriff of Crescent Cove and had just married her best friend Margaux.

"No. Of course not. But I did feel sorry for him. I thought maybe one of Crescent Cove's finest might give him a ride to where he's going. Not you, but Finley or Joe."

"Sure. One of them is bound to be out that way. We've got plenty of calls coming in. The weather isn't letting up much. The snow is supposed to pass through by the morning, but the temperature will drop. Is your heat working okay?"

"Yes. Thank you. Though we've pretty much moved downstairs to keep the heating bill down."

"If you want to come stay with me and Margaux and Connor until it warms up, you're welcome."

"Thanks, but we're fine so far. We're coming over tomorrow for a play date. Will we see you for dinner?"

"I hope so. Uh-oh, gotta go. I'll put someone on your hitchhiker. See you tomorrow."

He hung up. Bri dropped the cell on the table and opened the fridge to see what she could make for dinner.

DAVID HENDERSON HAD had enough. Not that he'd expected the car to pick him up. He'd learned that people weren't as giving or as tolerant or trusting as they had been when he left the States over ten years before. Except for a few quick holiday trips, he hadn't been back, and he was having trouble adjusting now.

But he'd made a promise. A promise he would keep. One that had kept him going for the last few months. Some days he wished he'd never gotten involved with the troubled soldier who had been in charge of bringing supplies to the Afghan village where they set up a medical triage tent for the local inhabitants.

He'd been pretty depressed himself that day and didn't really have the energy for someone else's problems, but the haunted look in that soldier's eyes . . . David recognized it and knew where it would invariably end up if the man didn't get help.

He shuddered from the cold and brushed away the snow that was gathering on his eyebrows.

A half hour ago he'd been dropped off at the highway exit to Crescent Cove, Connecticut, certain that a beach town would have a bunch of motels to choose from. So far he hadn't even seen an open gas station.

He had no idea how much longer it would take him to reach town. Where was sprawling urbanization when you needed food, warmth, a cup of coffee?

He shifted his backpack on his shoulders, shoved his gloved hands deep into the pockets of his field jacket and trudged ahead.

Across the road and through the bare trees he saw a dim light. Some happy family sitting toasty in their kitchen with their stainless steel appliances and granite countertops, while his feet were numb with cold. He felt a little envious. But only for a second.

They'd have a shit fit if he knocked on their door and asked for food, a bed, even a ride to the nearest hotel. But maybe they had a garage or a shed where he could at least get out of the snow and wind.

He set off across the road and slipped and slid down into a pasture where a few sparse winter stalks rose above the accumulating snow. He was careful not to get too close to the light ahead. He didn't want to get shot. And wouldn't that be a kick. To make it for years in hot spots around the world and take a bullet in the suburbs of Connecticut.

He came to a line of trees, their bare branches dimly lit from the reflective snow. And saw that he hadn't even reached the suburbs, but a dilapidated two-story farmhouse. But where there was a farmhouse there was bound to be some outbuildings. His night was beginning to look up.

He carefully skirted the source of the light that appeared

to be coming from a kitchen window. He could see a vase of some sort sitting on the sill. And he realized that the snow was beginning to taper off. That was a relief.

He could also make out the shape of a barn. With any luck there would be clean straw, a horse blanket, or a warm animal. And it was cheaper that the Holiday Inn.

Keeping to the shadows, David crept up to the barn. He'd be gone before morning. They'd never know. He'd learned the hard way how not to leave a trail. And now that the possibility of rest dangled like a carrot in front of him, David could barely keep on his feet.

By the time he reached the side door of the wooden barn he was staggering. He pulled at the door. And stepped inside to total dark.

BRI AND THE girls spent the night on an air mattress in the great room, surrounded by a barricade of pillows and covered with several down comforters. Mimi and Lily had not yet learned to sleep alone. And Bri couldn't stand to hear their cries the few times she attempted to put them to bed in the small bedroom just a doorway from her own. She knew they would have to learn, but they already had so much to get used to.

Hell, they couldn't even articulate their needs, though they had picked up quite a few words of English since Bri had brought them home. They were doing a lot better with English than she was doing with Chinese.

Nick had called to say they'd checked on the hitchhiker

but didn't find him. "Probably picked up by some generous soul. Hope they didn't make a big mistake."

"Nick, you cynic. It's Christmas," Bri said.

"Fine, but don't you ever pick up any hitchhikers."

"Yes sir, Chief."

"Huh. See you tomorrow."

Bri lowered herself to the floor and slipped beneath the covers.

When she awoke at daybreak, she felt the girls' bodies spooning against hers, and her love for them swelled as if they had been hers from the moment they breathed life. As if they were her own birth children. She lay for just a minute relishing the comfort of knowing they were a family, the sense of quiet trust.

Then she eased away from them, rolled over and stiffly got to her feet. She brushed her hair and teeth even though she was only going out to feed Hermione, the goat, and the chickens, and put out water for the cats who seemed to multiply from day to day.

She pulled on quilted snow pants over her pajamas, shrugged into a down jacket that she'd picked up at a consignment shop. Twisted her hair into a knot and tucked it into the hunting hat with earflaps that she wore to do chores. She never put it on without grinning.

If her friends could see her now . . . Except her real friends—the ones who stuck by her from her meteoric rise in the fashion runway world to her ignoble plunge to depression and despair, her painful climb back to where she was now— those friends saw her all the time in all manner of dress, in good moods and bad. They loved her anyway. The others? To hell with them.

Making one last check that the girls were still sleeping, Bri let herself out the back door. It had snowed over a foot during the night, but her menagerie would be hungry and she couldn't wait for the snow plow. She was one of the last stops on his route.

So she trudged through the knee deep snow, slowly so as not to slip or fall, carving out a path to the barn with each step. She was breathing hard by the time she reached the barn. She walked around to the side door, which was sheltered from the worst of the drifts. She grabbed the handle with both hands and tugged the door open.

Light was just filtering down from the loft windows, slashes of it seeping through the cracks in the wood. Bri smiled, feeling content and almost happy. She wished she could describe the feeling the dim light gave her. Her friend Margaux could design a dress called Barn at Sunrise, or something even more fanciful to add to her beach-inspired fashion line.

But Bri didn't have a way to express what she felt. She took courses, learned how to build a business, fix a leak, change a flat tire. Things she would have scoffed at in her younger years.

She lifted the metal lid of the storage bin, scooped out Hermione's morning ration of feed into a feed pail and carried it over to the corner of the barn where Hermione lived during inclement weather.

Hermione met her with a nasally *baa*.

"Morning, Miss Thing." Bri scrubbed the scruffy fur above her tail, and Hermione wiggled in response. She was old and no longer gave milk, not that Bri would have wanted to milk her. A girl did have her limits. She'd inherited Hermione from the owner when she bought the farm, and Bri felt responsible to make her last years comfortable. Hermione seemed totally willing to accept her new situation and her new mistress.

Bri hung the pail where the goat could reach it and went back across the barn for the pitchfork. As she reached for it she saw something move in one of the empty stalls. She grabbed the pitchfork in both hands. She'd never be able to outrun a wild animal. But she kept the doors and windows latched. If this was a predator, it was of the human variety.

She peered into the stall, pitchfork at the ready. Saw the end of what appeared to be a blue nylon sleeping bag and the bulk of someone sleeping inside. A thief? Murderer? Homeless person? Did they have homeless people at the Connecticut shore?

Whoever it was stirred, rolled over, taking the bag with him. Bri began to back cautiously to the door. But before she could reach it, Hermione tossed her head and knocked the feed pail off the hook. It clattered to the floor, only slightly muffled by the layer of straw.

It was enough to bring her squatter upright. Her first response was to scream. It looked like one of those Halloween coffins where the skeleton popped up and let out a maniacal laugh. The sound this guy made was more like an elephant grunt. And he looked like a yeti, encased in a dark green jacket. A black knit hat was pulled down over his forehead; the rest of his face was hidden behind an incipient beard.

"Sorry," he grunted out in a gravelly voice.

Bri clutched the pitchfork and tried to think.

"Sorry," he repeated. "I'm leaving." He pulled both arms out of the sleeping bag and lifted them, hands by his ears. "I'm harmless. Just needed a place to sleep."

He didn't sound like a derelict or an ax murderer. His voice, as it recovered from sleep, sounded more human, even friendly. And the thought of him sleeping in her barn all night dug at her sense of compassion. A bad thing. She steeled her heart. Brandished her pitchfork.

"Then you'd better get going. Or I'll have to call the police," she added for good measure.

The man scrambled to his feet. Then stopped, turned to look at her.

"I mean it." She jerked the pitchfork for emphasis. How stupid could she be? Standing here holding a stranger at bay with a pitchfork. It was too much, her mouth curved into a grin. It seemed to frighten her intruder. Well, good.

He inched away from her. "Actually, maybe that would be a good idea. I'm not dangerous, not a felon. I just couldn't find a motel between here and the highway. The police might be willing to give me a ride to Crescent Cove. Is it very far?"

"A couple of miles, but I don't know if—" She broke off. She'd almost told him that the roads wouldn't be cleared yet. Which meant she'd be stuck in the barn with this man and totally at his mercy.

"Or maybe you could just help me with some information. I'm looking for a guy named Nick Prescott. I was told he lived in Crescent Cove."

He was looking for Nick? For what?

"Do you know anybody by that name?"

"What do you want with him?"

"You do know him."

"I didn't say that."

"Look, I've come halfway across the country to find this guy. Can you just tell me if he's here or not?"

Bri deliberated. "He's the chief of police."

He expelled a deep breath that created a cloud in front of his face. "Is there another one? This man's a history professor. Or at least he was. I had his address in Denver. His college said he'd moved to Crescent Cove, but they wouldn't give me his new address."

"Nick was a professor. He's the interim chief. Why do you want to find him?"

He scowled beneath his knit hat. "I have a letter for him."

"A letter," she said incredulously. "Why didn't you just mail it?"

There was silence, then he said, "It's not that kind of letter."

A dozen things flashed across Bri's mind. Bill collector? Police business? Something about Connor, Nick's nephew, whom he and Margaux were in the process of adopting. Should she tell him where to find Nick?

She shivered and realized she was getting cold. The guy was shivering, too. It was damn cold, even in the barn. She wanted a nice hot cup of coffee. She did not want to be standing in the semidarkness of the barn, verbally fencing with a stranger.

She gripped the pitchfork, shifted her weight to both feet.

The stranger sighed. "It's from his brother."

"Ben?"

"Yes." He stepped forward.

Bri brandished the pitchfork but felt a little foolish. This man knew Ben—had known Ben. Ben was dead. Killed in Afghanistan.

"What's your name?"

"David. David Henderson. Do you mind if I put my boots on, my toes are getting numb."

Bri glanced down at his feet. Gray socks, a hole in the toe. He'd get a blister for sure if he walked very far with that rubbing his skin.

"Go ahead." Bri shifted the pitchfork. She really wanted to put it down and call Nick. The guy knelt down, pulled his gloves off and went about pulling on his boots. He had trouble getting the laces tied. His fingers were probably stiff from sleeping all night in the cold. Could you get frostbite sleeping in a barn in a sleeping bag?

He finally finished and stumbled to his feet. "Could you make that call? I'm kind of cold and a heated squad car is looking like the Ritz about now."

She could make the call, but she'd have to go back to the house to make it, she'd left her cell phone inside. She didn't exactly need it while she was feeding and watering the animals. And she still had the chickens to do.

But to do that she had to turn her back on him. Hell, how

had this happened? She should put a lock on her barn. And she would first thing tomorrow. But for now . . .

"Stay right where you are. I have to feed the chickens, then I'll call."

He crossed his arms, she was pretty sure she could hear his teeth chattering.

"Don't move." Keeping him in her sight, she made a crazy sideways walk to the feed box. She needed both hands to open the box and scoop out the chicken feed. She glanced back, making sure he was right where she left him, deliberated for a second, then reluctantly put down the pitchfork.

Chapter Two

· · · · · · · · ·

DAVID WATCHED THE woman move across the barn. She was tall; at first he thought she was a man. Once he got over the pitchfork aimed at him, he realized it was a woman's face nestled between those earflaps. And a damn good-looking one from what he could see. Of course looks could be deceiving. Which was beside the point.

She had to turn her back to him to open the feed box, and if he'd been thinking with half a brain, he would have made his escape then. But he wasn't. His brain was frozen along with the rest of him. He wanted heat, breakfast, a strong cup of coffee, a bathroom. As soon as he delivered this damn letter to Nick Prescott, he'd find a hotel room and sleep until he woke up. Then he'd decide where he was going next.

She finally relinquished the pitchfork and braced it against a wooden paddock. The barn was large, had several stalls, and must have housed a stable full of horses at one time. Now there only seemed to be a goat and a few chickens that he could here rustling and squawking at the other end of the barn.

She scooped up a pan of feed and hurried toward the chickens. And that's when he noticed the slight hitch to her walk. Where was her husband while she was out here doing chores? Sleeping? Working in town? Deployed? Dead? Divorced? Or just plain lazy and waiting for David with a shotgun at the door?

He shook himself, his mind was wandering, from cold, fatigue, from lack of sleep, from hunger. He shivered violently. "Y-Y-You need help?"

"No. Just stay there." Her voice echoed from the shadows. It was deep and throaty. A voice that could make you forget your manners. He wondered what she looked like beneath all that padding.

He clamped down on that thought. *Remember the husband with the shotgun.*

She finished up her chores then started back toward him. Stopped, turned around and grabbed her pitchfork. And he got a flash of American Gothic and decided he probably shouldn't wait around to see what she was married to.

But damn, he was cold. And he could barely feel his feet. He could die of exposure waiting here for her to finish her chores.

"L-Listen," he said through chattering teeth. Suddenly he was shivering uncontrollably. At least ten hours in subfreezing temperature, sleeping bag or no, had not been good.

"Jesus, you're freezing." She looked concerned but still wary.

"If you could just call the cops. I could use a warm place to stay even if it's a cell." He tried to smile, to reassure her, but he couldn't make his mouth move.

"Oh, crap," she said, her eyebrows frowning beneath her hat. "Can you promise me you're not crazy or a psychopath or anything?"

"I promise."

"Ridiculous, I know. If you are a psychopath you'd have no compunction about lying."

"Wh-Where did you get this f-fascination with psychopaths?" he asked. "There are not as many as television would lead you to believe."

"How would you know?"

"Statistics. But you don't have to believe me. Just make that call so I can leave you in peace. I'd walk into town but I can't feel my feet."

"Oh shit." She walked up to him, her limp less pronounced now, and gestured with that damn pitchfork. "You can wait in the mudroom while I call." She pushed that pitchfork at him again and he had to resist the temptation to pull it out of her hand. She was afraid and he didn't want to frighten her more. Maybe there was no husband waiting in the house. Maybe she was alone. She had every right to be afraid. But not of him.

"Thanks." He quickly shoved his sleeping bag into his backpack and threw it over one shoulder.

"Go out the side door." She motioned with the pitchfork. If he hadn't been so cold, he would have been offended. He headed toward the side door, pushed it open and stepped out into sun. He blinked against the glare off the snow, then shut his eyes, opening them little by little until he could stand the light.

And the snow. There had to be two feet of it. His kingdom for a warm bed and a hearty meal that didn't include yams, goat, or barley water. A gust of wind kicked snow in his face. The house looked a hundred miles away. He could barely make out footprints as the top layer of snow swirled with the wind like a living organism.

"Head for the side door," she said.

He started off toward an SUV parked by the side of the house. She stayed behind him like some dumb cowboy in a old television show. He was beginning to get annoyed. He glanced back.

She'd fallen behind a bit and was having difficulty getting through the drifts. He considered going back to help but decided not to tempt getting pitchforked. It might rip his field jacket. Or part of him.

Her head was down. All her attention was focused on making it through the snow.

He saw it coming and couldn't do a thing about it. Her foot slipped and after a wild moment of trying to regain her balance, she fell head first into the snow, still holding the pitchfork. Luckily it missed its owner.

For an instant he considered leaving her there long enough to ransack her kitchen for food and get the hell down the road. But his better self reined him in and he made the slow ponderous turn back to where she was struggling to get up.

As he reached for the pitchfork, she looked up at him, a zap of energy from clear blue eyes, full of challenge, anger, though whether at him or herself was hard to tell. And along with those two emotions, he saw something else, a flicker of fear.

He hesitated. "Hey," he said. "I'm one of the good guys." At least he'd tried to be.

He held out a hand to help her up. She just looked at it for a moment and finally took it. With David pulling and his captor pushing with the pitchfork, they managed to get her to her feet. He suddenly noticed how rosy her complexion was. Probably from exertion or embarrassment.

She was tall, David was taller. And he was getting tired of being prodded with an oversized fork. He extricated it from her hand and struck off toward the house and warmth.

"Hey," she yelled, fighting to keep up with him. "You have to wait for me."

David would have smiled if he could get his lips to move. As it was, he just kept trudging onward.

She lunged after him, pitched forward again. David gave it up. He tossed the pitchfork and his backpack onto the porch and went back to help her.

This time when he pulled her to her feet, he didn't let go. While she was getting her balance, he threw her over his shoulder and plodded toward the house.

"Put me down. Are you nuts?" She squirmed and kicked and they both nearly went down.

"No, but I might be a soprano if you keep kicking like that."

Her boots stilled. A few ponderously heavy yards later he deposited her on the kitchen porch.

"Thank you," she said between clenched teeth, but he thought she did that to keep them for chattering. He knew he was losing enamel, the way his were banging together.

"And if you'll call off your dogs, or husband, or both, I think it would at least be a nice show of appreciation to offer me a cup of coffee."

He reached for the door and was startled to see two little Asian faces peering out the glass window at him.

The woman pushed past him and called out something that surprised him. She spoke in Mandarin or at least her version of it. The faces moved away. She opened the door and gestured him in.

David entered the house, and the heat that hit him was almost painful, but it was a blessed pain. He let out a relieved sigh as he stood at the threshold and looked around. The children had disappeared.

"Do you mind if I get out of these shoes and coat?"

The woman was already shedding her jacket to reveal a pink flannel pajama top. "Crap," she said as she realized he was watching her. She quickly shed her boots, revealing red and white striped socks with toes. She yanked off her hat, and long blond hair fell past her shoulders.

Damn. Damn and damn.

"You can take them off but don't leave this room."

"Yes ma'am."

She ran past him still wearing her snow pants, which he

surmised covered pink flannel pajama bottoms. He began removing his gloves; heard more execrable Chinese from the other room. He removed the rest of his outerwear and found a bathroom where he cleaned up the best he could and went back into the kitchen to find a coffeepot. Hopefully, she'd let him have a cup before the police came.

He searched the fridge and cabinets while his toes and fingers burned as the circulation returned. He found a fine grind espresso in the fridge and was dumping it into a coffeemaker, finally feeling warmer than he had in the last twenty-four hours, when he heard someone behind him.

He turned, the coffee scoop arrested in air. Christ Almighty, she was beautiful. She'd tied that amazing hair back into a low ponytail. In jeans and a sweatshirt, she appeared incredibly tall and thin. He frowned at her, trying to figure out if she was really the same woman who'd held him hostage in the barn.

"I, um—" He held up the coffee scoop as explanation. His tongue felt too big for his mouth. Probably an early symptom of frostbite—or stupidity.

She came into the room, moving slowly, her gait smooth now. Gait? Hell, she wasn't a horse, she was a beguiling woman who exuded a kind of bewitching presence, like an actress or something. She was in her thirties, he guessed, though he'd never been that good at guessing women's ages. She didn't appear to be wearing makeup, but it didn't matter in the least, she had close to perfect features. Hell, except for that slight limp, she could have been a model.

"I see you've made yourself at home," she said.

"Sorry, I thought you could probably use a cup of coffee. I know I could."

She curled her lip at him. Ironically, it made her look more alluring.

He turned back to the pot and began dumping coffee into the filter. Poured water and turned the coffeemaker on. He knew he was taking a lot for granted from this woman. But he was cold, hungry, and just too tired of the whole mess to care.

He was like a horse sensing the stable, rushing to get this last duty fulfilled and head for home. Only he didn't have a home, just a barn for the night and a woman with a pitchfork.

The coffee started hissing.

"Did you get someone on the phone?"

"Yes. They're all busy. Bunch of downed power lines. Hell, you'd think it never snowed in Connecticut."

Chapter Three

· · · · · · · · ·

BRI STOOD REGARDING David Henderson's back. What the hell was she going to do with him? Now that he was inside, she couldn't very well thrust him out into the cold again. The kitchen window thermometer said it was twelve degrees.

A cold walk into town.

But he couldn't stay here.

"I told the dispatcher you wanted to talk to Nick. She asked your name. She'd never heard of you. She asked me what it was about. I told her I didn't know. She thought it was odd." And so did Bri.

"Look, I know you feel uncomfortable with me here. I don't blame you. I don't normally sleep in barns. I just couldn't find a hotel and it was dark and cold, and I was tired."

"So you said," Bri said, refusing to give in to his rationale. He could still be a psychopath, and she would have put them all at risk.

David had been frowning at her, but now he looked past her and smiled. Bri turned to see Mimi and Lily peering out from behind the doorway. That was one of the problems with the language barrier. She'd taken them to their room and told them to stay. For all the good it did.

"Zao shang hao," David said, in what to Bri sounded like perfect Chinese. Her suspicion barometer shot to the danger zone.

Mimi and Lily ran to Bri and hid behind her, but they peeked out at this new person, full of curiosity. She laid a protective hand on each little head and narrowed her eyes at him. Bri didn't believe in coincidences. She'd never had a vagrant sleep in her barn before. Never met someone looking for Nick. And on top of that spoke something that sounded like fluent Mandarin At least it did to her, whose grasp of the language was basic at best.

He spoke to them again, and the two heads nodded in Bri's palms.

"Did you just ask them if they were hungry?"

"Yes. It's morning, and I for one could use some breakfast."

"Where did you learn to speak Mandarin?"

"I know bits of lots of languages. I can say hello, order food, and ask the way to the American embassy in at least ten."

Bri couldn't help it, she smiled. Caught herself. "You're not a spy the agency sent to see how I'm treating the girls, are you?"

"No ma'am. Just a traveler who happened to stop for the night in your barn."

"How did you know Ben Prescott?"

His eyes hooded over. "I'll tell you over breakfast. I can't remember the last time I ate. Yesterday sometime, I think. Are your girls adapted to the new diet yet or shall we make congee and steamed eggs." He'd spoken the last words in Mandarin, and Mimi and Lily squealed and repeated "steamed eggs, steamed eggs," until Bri gave in and pointed him to the fridge.

"I don't suppose you're better at steaming eggs than I am."

David shrugged, opened the door and stuck his head inside. "Depends on how bad you are." His words echoed from inside the fridge.

The girls cautiously left her side and tiptoed toward the open fridge door. They squeezed in on either side of him and looked inside, too.

"I'm pretty bad, but they eat it . . . most of the time," Bri said, then realized no one was listening. And she had to fight off a little pang of jealousy when she saw how readily the girls were taking to this stranger as he handed the egg carton and a container of rice out to them.

Jealous and wary.

"Then allow me. I'm a pretty decent cook. It'll be pay for my night in your barn."

Bri acquiesced. That way she could keep an eye on him until Nick got here.

The kitchen began to fill with the aroma of cooking. David found a package of bacon in the freezer and was standing at the stove, stirring rice, turning bacon and popping bread in the toaster like a short order cook. Which, Bri realized, was entirely possible. A man hitchhiking cross-country probably had to pick up odd jobs where he could.

The windows had misted over and Bri and the girls drew funny faces on the frosted panes, but she still kept one eye on David while he worked.

At first she told herself she was making sure he didn't pull anything. But after a few minutes she just watched him as he moved from toaster to oven to fridge with a kind of choreographed grace, though he was a big man, tall, lanky, spare as if he'd been tempered in fire.

And when the hell did she start waxing poetic in the morning? She shook herself. Got up and began setting the table.

David announced breakfast, and the girls ran to their places, held their bowls in both hands and looked expectantly at him. It was one of the things Bri hadn't gotten used to. Their fear that there wouldn't be enough food for them.

It broke her heart every time. And she couldn't find the words to explain to them they would always have enough to eat, clothes to wear, a home. And all the love she could give.

She met David's eyes, saw that he understood, and she quickly looked away. She didn't want to share that deep, soul-twisting emotion. It was too dear, too precious, too personal.

And how did he know what she was feeling, anyway?

He took the girls' bowls, poured congee and eggs into them and took them to the table. Mimi and Lily followed close behind him, their mouths already open, like baby birds.

He went back to the stove, filled two plates with scrambled eggs, bacon, and toast and put them on the table. He motioned for Bri to sit, then poured two mugs of coffee and sat down across from her.

Bri's heart skipped several beats. It was a normal enough scene, played out in homes across the world. But not here. It would just be her and her girls. Every bad choice she had made in her life was because of a man, and after the accident that ended her career, she'd sworn to never let her fatal attraction be her downfall ever again.

Mimi and Lily finished eating. Bri had been paying too much attention to the stranger sitting across from her and they'd gulped down the food.

The girls had spent most of their lives worrying about getting food, and it was a hard fear to overcome. Usually she sat with them, reminding them to eat more slowly, telling them about lunch even when she hadn't thought about what she was making for lunch. But today she hadn't been paying attention and they looked a little confused.

"Tell David thank-you for your breakfast," Bri told them.

Lily happily obeyed, but Mimi kept her eyes on her bowl. Bri sighed.

"What's your name?" David asked Lily.

Lily straightened up and said, "Lee Lee."

"A very pretty name," he said.

"Lee Lee."

He chuckled and repeated his comment in Mandarin. Lily smiled.

He turned to Mimi, who ducked her head until her face was almost buried in her Princess Jasmine sweater.

David ducked down, too, tilted his head until he was on

the same level as her and could see her face. She glanced up at him from beneath jet black lashes.

"Do you have a pretty name, too?"

A tiny little nod.

"Let me guess. *Dia?*"

She shook her head, a tiny movement.

"Hmm. Not butterfly. Let's see. I've got it. *Hua.*"

Mimi looked up quickly, shook her head.

Bri wished she could understand what names he was saying. Hoped they weren't anything to make Mimi even shier and more frightened than she already was. Lily, being younger, had adapted to her new life faster than Mimi. The adoption agency people said this was to be expected. Mimi had spent more years in the orphanage than Lily. It was a life she was accustomed to, she knew no other, and it was harder for her to try new things.

"Wait, don't tell me." David frowned, knitting his eyebrows together. Then he smiled. "*Nangua?*"

Mimi pouted her bottom lip at him. But Bri could tell she was trying not to smile. "What does 'Nangua' mean?"

"Goose."

Bri smiled.

"Me Me Boy," Mimi whispered.

"Mimi boy?" David glanced a question at Bri.

"Boyce," she said, "Mimi Boyce."

"Ah, and that would make you Mama Boyce?"

Bri nodded.

"Well, Maomi. What is Mama's name?"

Mimi's pout reluctantly changed to a smile. "Bee."

"Bee Boy. Mama," David said.

"Mama," Mimi said.

"Okay, girls," Bri said. "Why don't you go turn on the television? Five minutes." She held up five fingers.

Both girls slipped off their chairs and hurried to the door.

"Hey," David said. "Lily and Maomi." He rattled off something that Bri couldn't begin to follow. He just knew how to order food and ask directions, her eye. The guy spoke pretty fluently.

Both girls immediately came back to the table, took their bowls over to the counter and placed them next to the sink.

"Thank you," he said, this time in English.

They smiled and ran into the great room. Bri listened for the sound of the television coming on. When she heard cartoon voices, she turned to David, not knowing whether she should be angry that he was trying to usurp her position with the girls or thankful for encouraging them to do more.

He took his plate to the sink and came back with the coffeepot.

"Thank you," she said. "For breakfast and for reaching out to my girls. And my name is Brianna. Brianna Boyce. Bri." She shrugged. "Or Bee." She smiled.

"Hmm. How long have you had them?"

"Since the beginning of November. About six weeks."

"They seem pretty well adapted."

"You think? It's been a giant learning curve. For all of us."

"You're doing fine."

"Is that the voice of authority?"

He huffed out a sigh that might have been a laugh.

"Hardly. I just wondered . . . Are you dong this alone, or is there a Mr. Boyce?"

"No there isn't."

"A significant other?"

She frowned at him. "No. And since I'm not intending to have one, I decided to adopt them myself."

"Hey. I wasn't making a judgment, just conversation."

"Who are you?"

He raised both eyebrows. "Just a guy trying to do what he said he would do and finding no room at the inn. Actually, not finding an inn at all. Nothing more or less."

"There are no hotels in Crescent Cove. A few B and Bs that open in the summer. But the motels are out on the highway."

"Not at the exit I came from."

"You hitchhiked here from where?"

"Most recently from the New Haven bus station. Met a guy driving up to Rhode Island and he gave me a ride to the Crescent Cove exit. Thanks to the kindness of some strangers. At least you didn't run me over last night."

"I—"

"I recognized the SUV. I don't blame you. You shouldn't pick up hitchhikers."

Bri shifted uncomfortably. She wasn't exactly afraid of him. Not anymore. But he seemed awfully . . . something. She couldn't put her finger on it. Though *at home* came to mind first. Followed quickly by *and not telling the whole truth.*

She reached for her coffee mug mainly just to have something to focus on. "You were going to tell me how you knew Ben Prescott."

He picked up his coffee mug. Held it in both hands. Looked into the dark liquid as if he might find the answer there.

"I met him in Afghanistan."

"I figured that much. Were you a soldier, too?"

"No, I was working . . . on an aid team there. Ben was leader of the squad assigned to provide escort to the supply convoy that serviced us." He stopped and frowned as if conjuring the image of their shared past and not liking what he saw.

A shiver shot up Bri's neck.

"We got to talking." He glanced up. "That's all."

"But he gave you a letter for his brother. Why?"

"A lot of guys did. You know, write a letter they hoped no one would ever have to send."

Bri cut back an unexpected sob. Embarrassed, she stared down at her hands clutching her coffee mug. "He was my first crush."

"Really? Was it . . . serious?"

She shook her head. "Only if giggling near the lifeguard stand is serious."

He smiled.

She hadn't meant to tell him that. "So he gave you this letter."

"Yes. I hoped I would never have to send it. But—"

She looked up. "But you did."

He nodded.

"But you brought it instead. And it's been a over year."

"You're awfully inquisitive."

"Listen. Nick Prescott is married to my best friend. They're raising Ben's child. We all knew Ben. I don't want anything to hurt them."

"Connor's here? Oh, good. Ben was worried about that."

"You know about Connor?"

"Yes. When I went to Colorado, no one seemed to know what happened to the boy. But I was hoping he was with Nick in Crescent Cove, so I came here. It's the best I could do for a friend." He fell into silence. Took a breath. "That's the story."

Bri's breakfast was suddenly sitting heavy in her stomach. "The letter. Ben didn't say anything bad, did he?"

"I didn't read it."

Chapter Four

....

Bri's cell phone rang. She looked at caller ID. Margaux. "Excuse me," she said, and hurried into the other room. "Hey."

"I just called to make sure you're okay. Nick called and said there was a man there looking for him."

Bri sheltered the phone with her hand and walked past the noise of the television toward the back of the house.

"He says he has a letter from Ben."

There was silence on the other end.

"I asked him why he didn't just send it. I think it's one of those if-you-read-this-I'm-dead letters."

"Why now? After all this time?"

"I asked him; he just said he had other things he had to do. He said he was working with some aid group over there, maybe he couldn't get away."

"I sure as hell hope Ben didn't do a final rant. Nick is just coming to terms with his death. If that's ever possible. But you know what I mean."

Bri didn't know the full story, but she knew Nick well enough now to know that he felt responsible for what had happened to Ben. Not just because he'd sent him to the army to keep him out of jail, but for not being able to be a father to him, when their father died.

"Nick is totally tied up with a multicar pileup on the other side of town. Have they plowed out by you yet? Why don't you come early and bring him with you. Nick will be more likely to swing by here than go out to your place, and I know he'll be crazed until he gets a chance to meet this Mr. Henderson." She sighed. "And so will I."

"They're not here yet. But I heard rumblings of plows in the distance. It shouldn't be too long."

"Good, I'll make lunch. The roads here are clear. One of the perks—the very few perks—of being married to the chief of police."

Bri smiled at the way Margaux always said "married" as if it were a magic word. And to see Nick and Margaux together after so much heartache and betrayal, Bri knew it was . . . for them. She felt a little envious. But not enough to start looking at men again.

She'd learned her lesson. And if she was ever in danger of forgetting it, it snowed or rained and the pain in her leg reminded her of why it was better to go solo from here on out.

"Do you feel safe with him in your house?"

"Yeah, but it's kind of weird. He speaks Mandarin."

"You're kidding. That's a strange coincidence."

"Yeah. And I don't believe in coincidences. The girls like him, though I'm not planning on turning my back on him for long, which means I'd better get off the phone."

"Good thinking. Call me every twenty minutes so I know you're okay."

"That might be a little obvious."

"I don't care. Call me."

"Okay. I hear the plows, but my service won't be here until later. I'll have to figure out a way to get to the snow blower and blow a path to the road without leaving the girls alone with him. I'll see you soon."

"Have him do it. Fair payment for a night in the Bri Barn Hilton."

Bri laughed. "I'll see what I can do."

She hung up and went into the kitchen. David was gone.

She quelled her first rush of panic. Probably in the bathroom. She tiptoed across the kitchen and looked down the hall. No sounds coming from the bath, but there were sounds coming from outside the kitchen door. She looked out.

He was outside, shoveling a path to her SUV. Was he being polite? Or was he as anxious to be gone as she was to have him go?

She went through the mudroom and stuck her head out the door. Her nose hairs bristled, it was so cold. "You don't have to do that," she called.

He stopped and leaned on the snow shovel. "In exchange for breakfast and a night in your barn." Each word was punctuated by a cloud of breath. "Besides, you'll need to get your car out to the road, and I need to get into town and clean up before I meet the police chief. I thought maybe I could bum a ride from one of the plow boys. They sound pretty close."

"I've got a snow blower in the garage. And I'll drive you to Margaux and Nick's if you can clear a path to the road. You can shower and whatever while I get the girls ready."

He grinned at her from behind his day old growth of beard, and Bri wondered if shaving was part of his clean-up agenda. He stuck the shovel in the pile of snow and looked around.

She pointed to the garage. "In there."

He touched his finger to his hat and trekked through the snow to the garage.

Bri went inside to help the girls get dressed, which they did quickly when they understood they were going to see Connor.

Margaux called again while David was in the shower.

"We're plowed out to the road," Bri told her.

"Good. I just put the mac and cheese in the oven. Mom's recipe. There's plenty. There's stuff for salad, so don't stop on the way. And I can rustle something else up for the adults, though I do make a mean mac 'n' cheese."

"And I open a mean box," Bri retorted. "Thanks, I'll take you up on it."

"I'll tell Nick to meet us here when he can."

Bri gathered up a change of clothes for the girls, some toys and their naptime stuffed animals, a bear and a rabbit that she'd brought to China and back again.

The three of them were sitting on the couch reading *Pokey Little Puppy* when David appeared, wearing jeans and a clean looking if slightly rumpled plaid shirt. The beard was gone. And Bri's heart skipped a beat at the transformation.

"Thanks. I feel almost human." He smiled, but his expression clouded. "I mean it. Thanks."

"No problem. Margaux invited us all to lunch. You're probably hungry after all that snow blowing. And the girls are always hungry." She gave them both a squeeze. "Coats," she said. "Connor's house."

They slipped off the couch and ran for the mudroom.

David followed them out.

The girls were halfway into their snowsuits and jackets, and David was stuffing things back into his backpack, when Bri got to the mudroom. He didn't look up. Just zipped the backpack, lifted it onto one shoulder and opened the door for them.

The girls climbed into their car seats and Bri fastened them in. David tossed his pack in the back hatch and got in the passenger side.

The girls chattered away, excited to see their friend Connor. Bri concentrated on driving and David looked out the window for the entire drive to the beach community where Margaux and Nick lived.

He'd been so engaged during breakfast, but now he seemed remote. Maybe he was worried about what the letter he was about to deliver said and how it would affect Ben's brother and the rest of his family. He might even be planning his escape if they decided to blame the messenger.

She wanted to reassure him that whatever the letter contained, they wouldn't blame him, but she knew that it would fall on deaf ears. David Henderson had withdrawn into his own world.

A few minutes later Bri pulled the car into the parking area at the back of the Sullivans' beach house. She and Margaux and their best friend, Grace, had spent so many wonderful summers there that just the sight of it made Bri relax.

She hadn't really been aware of just how tense she'd been until she saw her old friend smiling and running toward the car, pushing her arms into a huge orange parka that had to be Nick's. It clashed terribly with her nutmeg red hair.

Margaux glanced in the passenger side at David, nodded to him, then opened the door to the backseat to let Mimi out of her harness.

"Hi guys. Connor's so excited that you're here."

Lily was already trying to get out of her car seat when Bri opened the opposite door.

David got out of the car. Reluctantly, Bri thought. And who could blame him?

"Come on inside," Margaux said over her shoulder. "The heat's pumping and lunch is almost ready. And wait until you see our tree."

DAVID FOLLOWED THE others into a warm, friendly kitchen with old-fashioned wallpaper of watering cans and ivy. It reminded him of his grandmother's house. It was one of the few things he remembered about it or even his grandmother.

While Bri and Margaux were busy getting the girls out of their winter gear, a young boy in sweats and fleece-lined moccasins ran into the kitchen. He slowed down and looked at David, then continued out to the mudroom.

David stared after him. Dark hair and eyes, eyes David had seen before. He had to be Ben Prescott's child, Connor.

Why? Why hadn't Ben wanted to come back to this? His child. His family. Why had David agreed to keep his letter? Maybe if he'd refused to take it, Ben would have had second thoughts about what he was about to do.

He closed his eyes on the image of their last conversation. "What happens when the war is over?" Ben asked him, but it was a rhetorical question. "None of us can ever go back to what we were." That boyish smile. "In my case that would be a good thing."

David should have said, "There will be another war." There was always war in some place. Where the victims were mostly innocent. Where people like David with skills but without the supplies or equipment to use them, tried to clean up the mess. Whether it was mortar and bombs or the aftermath, when the weapons were gone and disease, hunger, and fear replaced them. But he didn't say any of that. Just "Okay."

"Is everything all right?"

He came back to the present. Tried to smile at Margaux Prescott, Ben's sister-in-law. She looked so concerned. Was it for him, a stranger? Or for her husband? This was going to be even harder than he expected. And at this point he already expected everything to be hard.

There was nothing good about war. Not loyalty, valor, heroics, camaraderie. It sucked. It killed. It maimed—

"David?" Bri said.

David started. He nodded toward Connor, who was dancing around the girls with cries of "Hurry up, slow pokes," while Mimi and Lily scrambled out of their boots and into their house slippers.

"He looks like his father."

"Yes, he does," Margaux said. "Let me take your coat."

He hesitated. He could drop the envelope on the table and leave. Pick up his backpack and walk to the nearest highway. Going north, south, west, it didn't matter. He wouldn't have to stay and see them react to whatever was in that envelope.

Maybe he should have read it first. Maybe he should have left well enough alone. Pretended that it didn't exist. They would never have known. But he couldn't do that. It might be the one thing that brought them closure. Acceptance.

He unzipped his jacket and handed it to her.

She took it with a tentative smile. "Why don't you guys go out to the parlor. See our first Christmas tree."

Yeah, c'mon." Connor motioned to the girls. Lily ran to him, but Mimi clutched Bri's hand.

"Can I come, too?" Bri asked.

"Sure. C'mon." Connor and Lily disappeared from the doorway, and Bri coaxed a timid Mimi out of the kitchen.

David felt a hand on his arm and he turned to see Margaux smiling at him. "David. You're welcome here. We appreciate that you've taken the time to come yourself. Especially now, during this season." She bit her lip. She was a lovely, poised woman, chic somehow in the old fashioned kitchen. It seemed weird to David to find two such sophisticated women living in a small town. Two beautiful women, obviously cultured, one alone in a dilapidated old farmhouse with two adopted children; the other in an old fashioned beach house married to a small town cop.

"Would you like some coffee or something?"

"No, thank you. I'll just—"

"Make yourself at home," she said as the oven buzzer went off.

David didn't offer to help. He knew he should, but he was disconcerted. The outsider in this strange but comfortable mix of people. He wished he could have known them without that letter hanging over them all. He wished the chief would get home, so he could deliver it and leave. He didn't belong here. Had no right to be here.

He had to fight the urge to run. Grab his coat and backpack and head for the highway.

Margaux took a large casserole dish out of the oven and put it on top of the stove. The smell of mac and cheese wafted toward him. So keen, so full of his own memories that he wanted to cry. But he hadn't cried in a long time.

"Let's join the others," she said, and steered him into a hallway toward the front of the house and a parlor where a ceiling-high Christmas tree filled one corner of the room, every inch decorated with eclectic ornaments and lights.

The girls sat on the floor while Connor pointed out the ones he'd made at school. Bri sat on an old trunk, listening just as raptly as Mimi and Lily.

"He used not to talk except in whispers," Margaux said quietly. "*He* found his way back."

David stared at her. Ben wouldn't be coming back ever. Or was she talking about him?

Lily climbed up into Bri's lap. Took her face in both hands. And started jabbering away.

"What, sweetie? What do you want?"

Lily pointed to the big gaudy star at the very top of the tree.

"A star like Connor's?"

Lily pointed some more. Slid down and ran to David. Talked to him so fast that he had a hard time not laughing.

"Tree," he said.

Her bottom lip stuck out.

"Tree," he repeated, and pointed to it. "Tell Mama."

Lily ran back to Bri. "Chee."

"Tree? You want a Christmas tree?"

"Chee. Me."

Bri laughed. "Okay. How about Mimi. Tree?" She pointed to Mimi, then Lily, then herself. "For us?"

Mimi nodded.

Lily ran back to the others. She and Connor jabbered away, each in their own language, neither minding that the other didn't understand what they were saying. At some point they would. Children were like that. Too bad adults weren't as smart.

He heard a door open and shut. Margaux left them. David suddenly felt cold in the cozy room. Nick Prescott was home. Footsteps crossed the kitchen, and David knew it as sure as he knew it was too late to chicken out now. A minute later a shadow fell across the doorway, and David came face-to-face with Nick Prescott.

Chapter Five

· · · · · · · · ·

NICK PRESCOTT WAS taller than his brother, bigger-boned, more strong-willed, and carrying a deep pain. David had seen that look in men's eyes before. He just hoped he wasn't going to make that pain worse.

Do no harm, he repeated to himself as he stepped forward to shake hands.

They exchanged names formally, like two businessmen at a board meeting.

David had already removed the letter from his pack and transferred it to his shirt pocket. He didn't want to have to fumble through what had to be an excruciating moment to the man who stood stoically in front of him. Not unfriendly, but preparing himself for whatever the letter contained.

He reached in his pocket and held out the folded envelope, hoping whatever it contained wouldn't prove too much for this man to take.

Nick took it. Looked at it. Glanced over to his wife, then turned around and left the room. Bri moved to Margaux's side. Margaux didn't attempt to go after her husband. Some things were best done alone.

Feeling like a harbinger of doom, David couldn't make himself move. He knew he should get his pack and walk away. But he had knowledge, stories, words that Nick Prescott didn't, and he felt the responsibility not to leave until he'd tried to make a terrible thing more understandable.

And then it would be over. He'd find a job somewhere. Working with his hands, but not anything where lives hung in the balance. Carpenter. Plumber. Mechanic. He'd learned a lot about a lot of things in the last decade. A handyman. A little of this and a little of that. The only blood, if spilled, would be his, from a cut finger, a scraped elbow.

He felt a tug at his leg. Lily shoved her scruffy bunny at him. He looked at her and she pushed it at him again. He took it. Knelt beside her and thanked her for sharing.

She reached up and squeezed his face in both hands.

His throat felt tight. "Bunny wabbit," he said.

She squealed with delight and pulled him toward the Christmas tree where Connor and Mimi were playing a mysterious game with colored blocks. They made room for him and Lily, and they all played. As far as David could tell, nobody knew the rules and nobody cared.

BRI STOOD AT the window next to Margaux and watched Nick stop by the lifeguard stand where Ben had spent so many summers. She put her arm around Margaux, and Margaux linked hers around Bri's waist. They didn't look at each other. Bri was having a hard time holding in her tears and her anxiety, and she knew if she looked at Margaux they would both lose it.

Margaux never told her what Nick had said about Ben's death, but she'd been around them both long enough to know that Nick felt responsible for it, and that it weighed him down in spite of Margaux and Connor and their love for him.

Nick's head was bent and Bri knew he was reading. Then he looked up and out to sea.

Margaux started.

"Go," Bri told her. "I'll watch the kids."

Margaux headed to the hallway, and David came to stand beside Bri at the window. A minute later they saw Margaux shrugging into a jacket as she hurried across the beach.

She reached Nick and he looked up. They stood looking at each other for what seemed like an eternity to Bri. Then he took Margaux in his arms and held her.

Bri blinked furiously. "That means everything is okay, right?"

"I don't know. But I don't think we should be watching." David nudged her away from the window.

"When are we going to eat?" Connor asked.

"Eat," echoed Lily.

Mimi looked up, expectant, anxious.

"Now," said Bri, forcing enthusiasm, then stood there unable to leave the window or take her eyes off the intimate, life-changing scene on the beach.

"Walk this way," David said, and lumbered bearlike out of the room. Lily and Connor jumped up and lumbered after him. After a quick look at Bri, Mimi ran after them.

Margaux came back in while the kids were eating.

"Nick had to check in at the station. But he's taking the rest of the day off. David, he wondered if you could stay and talk to him for a while."

"Is everything okay?" Bri asked, and held her breath waiting for Margaux's answer. David looked like a trapped man. And to all intents and purposes, he was.

"Well, yes. I think it is," Margaux said. "Considering. Let's eat. I'm suddenly ravenous."

Bri cleared the kids' meals away, while Margaux reset the table for three and made a plate for Nick that she put back in the oven. David stood off to the side, once again withdrawing from the situation. He was so strange, one minute playing with the kids, making breakfast, asking questions, the next, clammed up and retreating like maybe he wished he could disappear altogether.

She glanced over at him standing in the doorway, propped against the door frame. He should have looked relaxed now that he'd performed what he clearly saw as his duty, but he looked ready to bolt. *God, please don't let him be waiting to drop another bombshell.*

By the time Nick returned two hours later, Bri and Margaux were cleaning up after an hour of letting the kids decorate store bought cookies. Nick took two beers out of the fridge and he and David sat down at the kitchen table.

Bri and Margaux took the kids out to the parlor to watch

Rudolph, while Margaux plied Bri for information about David and his night in the barn. By the time they'd watched *Rudolph, Frosty the Snow Man, A Charlie Brown Christmas,* and were halfway through *The Grinch,* Bri's update was finished and Margaux and Bri had both begun casting surreptitious looks toward the hall door.

"What do you think they're talking about in there?" Bri said.

"I wish I knew. My guess is that David is telling Nick about knowing Ben?" Margaux grimaced. "I just hope he doesn't have any gory details. Nick doesn't need to deal with that, especially now when he's so busy."

"Surely he wouldn't put anyone through that. You don't think he witnessed what happened, do you?"

"I don't know. I hope not."

They turned back to the television.

They had just given in to pleas of *"Shrek, Shrek"* when Nick and David came into the living room. They both looked wrung out but calm, Nick, a man who had somehow been comforted and David as if he'd had a burden lifted.

David stepped toward Margaux. "I wanted to thank you for your hospitality." He glanced at Bri and she knew what was coming next. "And for *your* barn and breakfast. You both have great families."

It was an exit speech if Bri had ever heard one. And she wasn't ready for him to go. She cautioned herself to smile, say it was her pleasure and let him walk away. Hell, just this morning she couldn't wait to get rid of him. But now . . . she'd known him less than twenty-four hours and yet somehow he'd carved out a place for himself in their extended family.

She stood just as he said, "But I have to get going. Nick was kind enough to offer me a ride to the highway."

Margaux and Bri both zeroed in on Nick, who shrugged slightly.

"You don't have to go," Connor said. "We're going to build a snowman and have hot chocolate with marshmallows."

Sensing something was happening, Mimi and Lily stood up and ran to Bri, burrowing into her legs and looking up at her for answers. "It's okay," she said. "David has to go away." Bri looked to David to translate.

He did, then smiled at the girls, nodded to the room, leaving them as frozen as if he'd cast a spell.

Margaux broke it. "Are you hitching? Wouldn't it better to wait until tomorrow and get an earlier start? It will be dark soon."

Bri came to life. "And you might not find a barn as deluxe as mine."

David smiled. "I know for sure I won't find a roommate like Hermione."

"We can give you a bed for the night," said Margaux. "It's the least we can do, right, Nick?"

"Of course," Nick said, but he didn't seem too enthusiastic.

Was Nick anxious to get rid of him? What had passed between the two men during the last hour?

"Thanks, but—"

"And," Bri said, "if you liked the barn, you should see my caretaker's cottage."

"Does it even have heat?" Nick asked, and gave Bri a cautionary look. What wasn't he saying? Did he think David was not to be trusted?

"Yes, and electricity and running water. I've been using it as a workshop. Besides," she continued, "I was kind of hoping you could help me buy a tree with the girls tomorrow. And explain to them about Christmas."

IT WAS TEMPTING. He'd been alone for so long, he'd grown accustomed to it. Expected it. Craved it. Until now. But that had changed the minute Bri shoved that pitchfork at him. At his first sight of Lily and Mimi. At the spoken thanks and unspoken understanding from Nick Prescott. His wife's generosity. The decorated tree, the warmth and closeness of the group. They weren't even real family. Just a mash-up of stray ends. And yet they were everything David thought a family should be.

God, it was so tempting. And it was Christmas. He could help them buy a tree. Tell the girls about Santa Claus or whatever. Sit around the fireplace . . .

Then he thought about his last December. An epidemic swept over the village. The supplies were late, held up by warring factions. And all he could do was watch, first the children, then the old people die. He hadn't even thought about Christmas. He wanted to erase that memory. Maybe it was better to let Christmas become like all other days. Each the same as the next. Nothing to remember. Everything to forget. Burning the memory bridge.

He glanced at Nick. The man was no fool; he didn't trust David, and David didn't blame him. Only he knew himself well enough to know that he wouldn't run amok like some. He was here, wasn't he? He wouldn't lose it and hurt anyone. He'd burned out; disgusted with greed, corruption, the hatred, the uselessness, the inevitability of it all.

Afghanistan had just been the straw that had broken his back. He'd given up and come back to find Ben's brother.

Now that was done.

He realized that everyone had fallen silent and was watching him.

"Nick will tell you, Bri, that you shouldn't invite strangers into your home."

She put her hand on her hip and shot him an ironic look. "Well it's a little late for that. And the cottage is a good two hundred feet away." She turned to Nick. "I'll lock my door."

In the end he agreed to take up short-term residence in the caretaker's cottage in exchange for helping with the tree and chopping some firewood and doing any other chores that she needed done.

When he finally said yes, Margaux and Bri looked satisfied. Nick looked at him like he'd lost his mind, but he didn't say a word against the plan.

So after a snowman and hot chocolate with marshmallows, he and Bri bundled Lily and Mimi back into their snowsuits and headed back to the farmhouse.

"Oh good, my plow guys have come," Bri said as they pulled into a cleared drive. "I was afraid we were going to have to trek across the pasture."

She drove past the house, which was lit up with welcoming light. And down a narrow car path to the caretaker's cottage. It was a smaller, one-story version of the main house, sitting at the end of the path on a blanket of snow. It was separated from the main house by a stand of now leafless trees.

David wondered what it looked like in summer and was sorry he wouldn't see it.

"We'll get you settled, then go make something for dinner."

"You don't have to do that. Margaux stuffed me with food all day."

Bri laughed. "The Sullivans have always fed everyone. In the summer's we practically lived at their house. Margaux's mom, Jude, makes the best homemade lemonade. In the summer there's nothing better." She stopped. "Anyway, you won't get as good here, but you won't starve."

David didn't argue, though he was exhausted, not just from today, not even from his travel across the country. He was just tired. So damn tired.

Bri stopped the car, looked in the backseat, where Mimi and Lily had fallen asleep before they'd gone two blocks. David took his pack and followed Bri the short distance across the snow to the front door. Bri pulled off her glove with her teeth and held it in her mouth while she jangled through a key ring to find the one that opened the door.

It was endearing, how she went from sophisticated woman to farm girl. She opened the door and reached inside for the light switch. The lights came on, outlining a square room with a sofa and scrubbed wood table.

The room was cold, but not as cold as the barn, for which David was grateful. Bri crossed to another door and fiddled with a thermostat. Baseboard heaters began to crackle and pop.

Serious living accommodations.

Bri bent over and touched the front of the nearest one with her palm. "Whew," she said. "Now if the pipes haven't frozen . . ."

David dropped his pack at the door and followed her into a small kitchen with ancient appliances he had no intention of using. She turned on the sink. After a couple of bangs and a screech, water gushed out of the old spigot.

Bri turned a satisfied smile on him. "I had the cottage fitted out three summers ago. I stay here when the renovations in the house make staying there impossible."

"Does that happen a lot?"

"Yeah. It seems like the more work you do, the more there is to do." She turned off the water and went back into the main room. "You can sleep in here," she said, and disappeared into another room.

It was a bedroom, and already the heat was warming the space.

I'll have to get linens and blankets from the house, but I'm assuming you can make your own bed." She shot him a grin that made the room seem too hot.

"I've got my sleeping bag."

"Nonsense. It probably could use a spin through the wash, in fact you're welcome to use the washing machine in the house."

"The clothes I wore today were clean."

"Jeez, I was just being nice. Do what you want. Come on. I don't want the girls waking up and wondering where I am."

He meant to say he would be fine. That he would just stay here and be gone in the morning. But he didn't. "I'll take you up on the blankets." He left his pack inside the door and climbed back into the car.

Chapter Six

· · · · · · · · ·

BRI AWOKE THE next morning to sunshine and the smell of coffee. She squinted across the room to the clock. Nearly nine o'clock. The girls were still asleep. They were worn-out.

She had slept in her own room that night. Sometime during the night Mimi and Lily had climbed into bed with her, and now all three of them lay cuddled together under a mountain of blankets.

Bri rolled out of bed. Stood a minute to get the circulation going, then quickly dressed in jeans and sweater and her Uggs. For the briefest second she thought of all her former clothes stuffed in a closet upstairs. She'd thrown out most of her runway samples years before, but she still liked nice clothes, even though she had little opportunity to wear them. Now when she dressed to go out, she wore Margaux's designs.

Bri shook herself. Why the hell was she thinking about clothes when she had a boatload of stuff to do today?

She hurried out to the kitchen, where she found the coffee but no David. She did hear him. He was outside, chopping wood. The guy was too good to be true. And she knew well what seemed to be too good to be true invariably was. Still, she didn't mind having a store of firewood without actually having to do the work herself.

She started breakfast.

A few minutes later the back door opened, bringing a quick draft of cold air before it shut again. David stamped his boots on the mat and came into the kitchen. He stopped.

"Oh," he said as she handed him a mug of coffee. "You're awake."

"And making pancakes. I hope you like pancakes. It's something the girls actually like. Though I'm afraid it's the syrup that won them over."

"Syrup is the best part of pancakes," he said, glancing at the pan. "And the ears," he added.

"There supposed to be Mickey Mouse," she said.

Mimi and Lily padded into the kitchen in footed pajamas.

"'Morning you two sleepyheads," Bri said. "Breakfast is ready and then we're going to get a Christmas tree." Their first tree as a family. Bri couldn't believe her good fortune.

THE DAY WAS sunny and not quite so cold when they all climbed into the SUV and drove down the road to McGruder's farm stand. Even this early there were a number of cars parked in the lot. At the far end, several families stood in front of a white trailer, waiting for their trees to be netted and tied to their car roofs.

Bri parked the SUV and they made their way across the pavement to the tree lot. There was a forest of cut trees, short and tall, thin and fat, balsam and Douglas, Frazier and blue spruce, white pine. Mimi and Lily stood still looking around in fascination, their mouths slightly open.

Mimi pushed into Bri.

"Christmas trees," Bri told her. "Like Connor's tree."

"Chee," squealed Lily, and ran over to a skyscraper of a Frazier fir, at least ten or twelve feet high. "Chee."

"Yes, that's right, a Christmas tree. Lots of trees. Let's pick one."

They wandered up and down the rows, pulling out one, discussing the merits of another. Found one that seemed perfect.

"How about this one?" Bri asked.

"Chee," Lily said, and pointed behind them.

They all turned around and looked at the row of trees. "You like one back there?"

"Chee," Lily said, and ran back the way they had come. She stopped at the entrance. "Chee." She pointed up to the giant tree.

"I think Lili Boy has made up her mind," David said.

Bri considered. It might just fit beneath the ceiling. She looked at David. "You'll have to stay to help decorate the top."

He hesitated.

Bri played her last card. "I'll at least need someone to hold the ladder."

David remembered her limp in the barn, something he hadn't noticed since. She was pretty good at hiding it, except when she was in a hurry or in the snow.

"When were you planning on decorating it?"

"Today. At least we can make a start. I'm not sure I have that many decorations. I usually go much smaller, but what the hey."

"Chee," sang Lily. "Chee."

Bri knelt down by Mimi. "What do you say? Do you like this one?"

Mimi shrugged.

David asked her again in Mandarin.

She nodded.

They got someone to carry it and went to the trailer to pay.

Bri let go of Mimi to reach in her purse for her wallet; Mimi darted away.

"Mimi!" Bri ran after her and found her standing in the midst of the smallest trees.

"Honey, don't run away."

Her face went blank, she mumbled something.

Bri knelt down on one knee. "Say again."

"Chee," Mimi said.

Bri looked around. She and Mimi were head height with the surrounding Christmas trees. Mimi wanted a small tree, one her size. Bri could have stood up and sang the Hallelujah Chorus. Mimi was asserting herself at last.

Mimi picked her tree and Bri was carrying it out when David and Lily found them.

"I guess we're having two trees this Christmas," Bri told David.

While the tree man tied the trees up, they went into McGruder's farm store and bought several boxes of lights and two giant stars to put on top of the trees.

Then they carried the two trees home and put both in the parlor side by side.

After lunch, Bri went upstairs to the hall closet where she kept the ornaments. She pulled down a red and green plastic container and turned . . . right into David. She hadn't heard him come up the stairs. They stood there for a lifetime, each holding one side of the box, neither letting go.

"Thought you could use some help," he said, and took the container from her.

"I—yes, thank you." She relinquished her side of the box, torn between being grateful and being pissed that he thought she couldn't carry a box by herself. But she had nothing to prove. She'd taken care of herself for a long time, had practically refurbished the old house single-handedly, only relying on others for things she didn't know; plumbing, electricity, and heavy lifting.

Bri was proud, independent, and comfortable in her skin. And she'd learned a long time ago not to turn down help when it was offered. She smiled and reached into the closet for the second box.

Downstairs, Lily and Mimi were helping David put the container on the floor, then they knelt down beside it and peered at the top as if something magical might spring from it.

And something magical did. Bri opened the top to a strand of gold garland that formed a spiral on top of the other ornaments. Tiny metallic stars nestled in the shiny cellophane.

"I'll admit it, " Bri said after a raised eyebrow from David. "I like colorful ornaments. Some would say tacky. I say festive." She lifted out the garland and hung it around her shoulders. "Oh, Christmas tree, Oh Christmas tree." She looped it around the girls and the three of them held hands and circled, galloping and singing like mismatched dervishes until they fell down.

Laughing, Bri pushed back to her feet.

Mimi and Lily scrambled over to the container and looked inside again, so close that they bumped heads.

"Lights first." Bri collected the garland, tossed it on the couch, and opened the second container. She pulled out a tangled mess of miniature lights. "Oh, dear," she said, and placed them on the couch.

David reached in and pulled out another two strands more neatly tied.

"I forgot about those," Bri said. "But I'd better warn you. They blink."

David pulled out another and held it up. "Pink flamingos?"

"I thought they were cute."

David shook his head in mock dismay. At least Bri hoped it was mock. "The girls will love them," she protested.

"I'm sure they will. Who wouldn't?" He laughed and reached in for the last string.

"These are the best." Bri stretched them out. "Bubble lights. They're really going to love these."

While Bri and the girls untangled the strings of lights, David tested each strand for bare wires and missing lights, then began wrapping them around the large tree. Bri, with the girls holding onto the string, wrapped the little tree. They didn't let go until Bri took the ends out of their hands and said, "Watch." She plugged in the lights.

The tree lit up; Mimi jumped back, and both girls clapped their hands.

They could have stopped there and been perfectly content, but Bri was in full excess mode. She went back to the container of ornaments, began pulling out boxes of balls, bells, wooden figures, seashells, pinecones, jewels, and Moravian stars.

She carefully handed each of the girls an ornament and took one for herself, then showed them how to hang them on the branches. There was no stopping them now. They ran back to the container, dug into the next box, which held vintage cars and trucks, a sleigh, and several Santa figures, nestled in snowy white tissue paper.

When the tree was weighed down with enough ornaments for its much larger companion, Bri stopped them. "We have to save some for the other tree."

While David finished hanging the lights, Bri sat Mimi and Lily down at the old card table they used for crafts and dumped a bag of colorful construction paper strips onto the table.

She showed them how to glue the ends together, then

string the next strip through the circle and glue it, too. Piles of chains grew at their feet. Lily glued her fingers together and laughed. Next Mimi glued her fingers. When they tired of gluing each other, they turned on Bri and, each taking a hand, glued her fingers together. Fortunately it was Elmer's and didn't stick for long.

Simple pleasures, Bri thought as the girls manipulated her fingers and she watched David wind the strings of multicolored lights.

She wondered how long it would be before television and video games took the place of making paper chains and playing with clay. When potato chips and ice cream would replace rice and steamed eggs. Well, ice cream had already gotten a big head start. Cookies were a close second, and it was just a matter of time until the rest followed.

Bri looked forward to that time, and at the same time knew she would miss these tender first months where everything was an adventure, sometimes fun, sometimes frightening, but experienced together. She would make sure the girls were brought up in a loving but firm home.

Then maybe they wouldn't be inclined to follow in their adopted mother's footsteps. She didn't want them making the kinds of mistakes she'd made. Though she knew no matter how she tried to protect them, one day she'd have to let them go, just like her mother had let her go. All in all, it had turned out pretty okay, in spite of some serious missteps, but now her life was back on track. Better than on track; she had a family, friends, a home.

Soon she would have to register Mimi for school and

Lily for preschool. They'd buy school clothes and supplies together, then she'd send them off and . . . and make them snacks when they came home. She'd read to them at night, and *Pokey Little Puppy* would be replaced with *The Secret Garden, Little Women, The Hobbit*. Maybe they'd get a real puppy.

David climbed down from the ladder and stood back to regard his handiwork, and Bri felt an unsuspected pang. He would soon be gone out of their lives. He'd been here for two days. He didn't talk much about himself, but in other ways Bri felt as if she'd known him forever.

The girls both accepted him like they accepted the other changes in their lives. Would they miss him when he left? Would Bri?

He turned and their eyes met. He smiled. "Looks like you've lost two elves."

"What?" Bri looked down. While she'd been watching David, Mimi and Lily had fallen asleep among the paper chains. She smiled and reached for her cell phone. "A Kodak moment," she said, and took a picture. She took another picture of the trees.

She wanted to take a picture of him, but that seemed a little pushy even for her. Something told her he didn't want to be remembered. And she wondered why that was.

She pulled the afghan off the back of the couch and covered the girls where they slept.

"I'd better start dinner."

David followed Bri into the kitchen, where she heated soup she'd taken out of the freezer that morning.

"We're not starving you, are we?" she asked David. "You'd probably kill for a hamburger about now."

"Not at all, I ate my share of fast food on my way from Denver to here."

"Did you hitchhike all the way?"

"No. I took a bus most of the way."

She frowned at him. Was he broke? He must be, especially if he'd left Afghanistan and started looking for Nick right away.

"Do you have plans? Someplace to go? Are you going back to aid work?"

"No, to all three."

"What are you going to do?"

"Whatever comes my way. For starters, I'll set the table."

Mimi and Lily could hardly keep their eyes open during dinner. And Lily barely ate a thing. But when Bri announced bedtime, they refused to budge.

"Chee." Lily said. "Lili chee."

"Tomorrow," Bri said. "After breakfast and baths."

Mimi slid off her chair, but Lily didn't budge.

"Come on, Miss Stubborn."

Lily lifted her arms to be picked up. She whimpered when Bri shifted her to her hip, and when they reached their bedroom, Bri had to pull her arms away so she could put her down. Lily fell asleep on her princess bed while Mimi was still undressing.

The room was warm. Bri pulled the covers over Lily and lifted the guardrail. There were two identical beds in the room, but Mimi climbed in next to Lily, leaving her bed empty. Bri kissed her good-night and pulled up the other rail.

Mimi sat up. Reached for Bri. Bri hugged her and whispered, "Story?"

Mimi nodded, so Bri lowered the rail again and sat next to her to read *One Fish Two Fish Red Fish Blue Fish* until she fell asleep with her head on Bri's stomach. Bri eased her back down, covered her, and flicked on the night-light before she tiptoed out of the room.

When she returned to the kitchen, David had done the dishes.

"You didn't have to do that," she told him.

"You should accept help when you can get it. You have your hands full with those two."

"I wouldn't have it any other way."

"They're asleep?"

"Yep. And in their own beds. Well, they're both in Lily's bed. They'll crawl into mine before the night is through. Sometimes we sleep in the great room. On the floor. It's cozy."

"And warm."

"Yes. The heating has been brought to code, but we mainly stay downstairs to save on the heating bill. And to tell the truth, they don't like to be left alone." She shrugged. "Maybe I should be encouraging them to get used to sleeping alone, but I don't have the heart. Not quite yet."

"It takes as long as it takes. Just make the transition as easy as possible and do it before it becomes a new habit."

She frowned at him.

"Sorry," he said. "I'll mind my own business."

"Don't be, but that sounded like the voice of authority."

"Not me. Just something my mother used to say."

"Your mother?"

"Yeah." He hesitated. "My parents were . . . kind of missionaries."

Missionaries? Bri rapidly went back through their conversations to see if she had made any cracks about religion or used any dirty words. She didn't think so. She was much more careful now that she was a mother. "And you're a—"

David laughed. "Don't worry, I'm not. I'm not even a believer. It's just the reason I know a little about a lot of stuff."

"And why you speak so many languages. And why you help people in need."

He lifted one shoulder in a semblance of a shrug. "Mainly I waded through a lot of red tape, argued with frightened locals, and got pissed off a lot. But I did learn a few words and phrases."

"Still . . ."

"It's been a long day. If you can manage, I'll get going to my deluxe accommodations." His face clouded over. "Thanks. You didn't need to be so kind."

He headed for the door.

"You want a cup of coffee before you go? I might even be able to rustle up a bottle of wine."

He hesitated. Considered, then came back. "Sure."

She reached into the fridge and came out with a bottle. "I don't drink much these days. And I don't have any beer. But I've been waiting to drink this." She looked at the wine bottle's label. "White, dry. Do you like wine?"

"Good enough. Where's the corkscrew? I'll open it for you."

She pulled open the utility drawer, fished out the corkscrew, but kept it. "You haven't stopped doing stuff since you walked through that door yesterday morning. Take a load off. I'll open it."

"Am I being pushy?"

"Nope, you're making my life ten times easier, but I don't want to take advantage of you." *And I don't want to get used to it.*

"You're used to doing things for yourself."

"Yes, I am." She laughed. "Now that I have a bunch of friends always ready to help me out, I find that I don't want to use them unless I have to."

"Use them?"

"I didn't mean it like that. I used to use people all the time. Not anymore."

"How did you hurt your leg?"

"Is it that obvious?"

"Only in the barn yesterday and in the snow."

"When I hurry or get off balance." She handed him the corkscrew. "Open the wine and I'll tell you."

Chapter Seven

....

"AND THAT'S THE story." Bri stretched back on the couch and watched while David poured her another glass of wine. "Fast living, drugs, drink, a guy driving too fast, and this runway model woke up in a Paris hospital, crippled in mind and body, unemployed and unemployable."

"Would I still find your name if I Googled you?"

Bri shrugged. "I don't know. I don't look. Sometimes you really can't go back again."

"Would you if you could?"

Bri thought about it. It was a question she never asked herself. And now that David had asked it, she realized she had known the answer all along.

"No. It was a great gig and I'm glad I had the chance to do it. But I would have had to retire a few years later anyway. Models these days get started around fourteen and are in their prime before they hit twenty."

"Whew. I had no idea. Actually, I never thought about it. I'm not much into fashion."

"I can tell." She laughed at his expression. "Fashion does not make the man, no matter what the ads tell you. Take Nick Prescott, totally clueless about how to dress. Margaux, before she moved back to marry Nick, was a major designer in New York."

"What's with this town? Is everyone an ex-famous person?"

"Not by a long shot. But it is a place to fix broken lives, build new lives, and dream new dreams. It's got a fantastic diner. You'll meet Dottie at Margaux and Nick's on Christmas day . . ." She paused, glanced at him. "If you're still here. And for the three months of summer, we're a real cosmopolitan mash-up," she said more brightly. "The summer houses open up and there's an influx of tourists. Most locals work their butts off during the season, then relax again after Labor Day.

"Kind of the best of both worlds." She stifled a yawn.

David stood. "I'll let you get to sleep. I—I'll see you in the morning."

He grabbed his glass and headed for the kitchen.

"David," Bri said.

He stopped, turned around.

"I didn't mean to make you feel pressured to stay for Christmas, but you're welcome if you decide you'd like to share it with us. Everyone will be glad."

"Thanks. Good night." And he was gone. Bri sat where she was until she heard the back door close. Waited until he had time to reach the caretaker's cottage, then she began turning off the lights.

DAVID TRUDGED TOWARD the cottage, the rime of snow crunching beneath his boots. It wasn't her invitation to stay for Christmas that had rattled him. It was her description of Crescent Cove. *A place to fix broken lives, build new lives, dream new dreams.*

But not for the likes of him, a man who walked away from his job, his avocation, from the people who needed him, from his responsibility and promise to help them.

But he had nothing left to give. Ever again. To anyone. Any illusion he might have of finding meaning in his life was gone. The job was just too big, too difficult, too overwhelming, and just damn depressing.

What vindictive God had led him here, to this woman and these children? To a son who would never know his father. To a man who shouldered his responsibility and didn't complain. He knew those kind of men. Had seen them come and go. Had thought for most of his life that he was one of them.

And the longer he stayed here, with all this talk about welcome and fixing broken lives, the longer he was kept from admitting his failure. And finding a place to land.

He'd pack tonight and leave tomorrow. It was the best way, before he started thinking about trying once more to make a meaningful life for himself. Make himself meaningful to others. Maybe someday he would find some kind of acceptance, but not here, not now. He'd given what he could give and he had nothing left.

He threw his backpack on the bed, shoved his few clothes and belongings into it and fastened it. Pushed it to the floor and lay down on the bed fully clothed. At first light he would walk away. Leave a note and go. They would forget him soon enough.

BRI AWOKE WITH a start. She was in her own bed, alone. Then she heard what had awakened her. Someone was crying. One of the girls. She sat up, looked at the clock. Three o'clock. She pushed the covers away and hurried next door.

Mimi slept, but Lily tossed in her sleep, pushing the covers away. Overstimulated, Bri thought, too much excitement with the tree and the decorations and having David around. She should have taken more time with them before bed tonight. But they'd barely been able to stay awake. Lily had fallen asleep before Mimi even got into bed.

Lily moaned, and Bri sat down on the edge of the bed and put a hand on her back.

"Mama's here, Lily. Mama's here."

"Mama," Lily whimpered.

"Right here, beautiful girl. Mama's right here." She ran her hand lightly over Lily's back. She seemed warm. Maybe she'd gotten too hot under the comforter.

Bri pulled it away and straightened the sheet that had become twisted during Lily's tossing.

She started to sing, quietly in her deep contralto, "Hush little baby don't say a word . . ." Lily stilled, seemed to sleep. Bri covered her again, this time with a lighter blanket, and tiptoed out of the room.

She'd barely drifted off again when a high piercing scream rent the air. This wasn't normal. Not even when the girls had nightmares had they screamed like that. The scream turned into a cry; was joined by another cry. Mimi was awake and crying, too.

The cries became hysterical, and Bri panicked. She nearly fell out of bed, stumbled to the next room, dragging her weak leg rather than waiting for the circulation to return.

Mimi sat straight up in bed wailing. But they were both safe, and Bri castigated herself for that momentary betraying fear that David had come back in the house and was a psychopath after all.

Lily flailed now, tossing from side to side, holding perfectly still and screaming again to restart the process. Bri turned on the light and rushed to Lily's side of the bed. She was flushed. Bri touched her forehead. She was burning up.

"It's all right, baby." Bri gathered Lily into her arms. Mimi continued to wail, rocking back and forth, her eyes wide and unseeing.

Lily tried to push Bri away.

Was it the flu? But this wasn't an ordinary flu. Why was she screaming as if she were in pain?

"Lily, what hurts?"

Lily cried out words, but the only one Bri could understand was *mama*.

"Show Mama what hurts." She tried desperately to remember the Chinese word for pain. Her mind went blank.

Baby Tylenol to bring down the fever. But as Bri let go of Lily she let out another piercing scream. She should take her to the hospital, but Lily wouldn't even be able to tell them what was wrong.

But David could. He would understand. And then she would know what to do.

"Mimi, please stop crying and look after your sister. I'm going to get David."

Mimi kept crying but crawled to sit by Lily, who had suddenly gone very still.

"No!" cried Bri. Reached for Lily, and Lily moved beneath her hand. Bri shuddered out a breath.

"Stay," she told Mimi. She ran for the mudroom, pulled on boots, grabbed her coat, and raced toward the caretaker's cottage.

There was a light coming from inside. She didn't stop to question why David would be up at this hour. She zeroed in on the light and concentrated on not falling down on the icy snow.

She was out of breath by the time she reached the cottage. She threw herself at the door. Knocked. "David!" Hesitated only a second and knocked again. Called out. Where was he? "Lily's sick! I can't understand her. David!" She pounded on the door with both fists . "David! Damn you, open the door!" The last plea ended in a sob. "Please," she said, and fell against the door.

It opened and she almost lost her balance.

He was dressed but looked dazed. She grabbed at him. "Lily's sick. You have to ask her what's wrong. She just screams when I try to move her."

He just stood there, and for one horrible moment she was afraid he wouldn't help.

Then he took her by both arms. "Pull yourself together. I'll get my coat."

If the cold night hadn't sobered her, his words did. She took a breath and turned back to the house. Before she got far, David was by her side, had laced his arm through hers. "Just lean on me. And fill me in."

Lean on him. At this point she would welcome someone to lean on. She must have been crazy to think that she could raise two girls with whom she couldn't even communicate.

"Bri. What are her symptoms?"

Bri jerked. "I heard her crying. Sometimes she does. She seemed a little warm, but she went back to sleep. Later she screamed again and when I went to see, I realized she was burning up. I was going to give her some Tylenol but I wasn't sure. I asked her what was wrong. I couldn't understand her. I couldn't understand anything. I couldn't remember any word of Mandarin. Oh God. What's wrong with her?"

"Come on. We'll take a look, okay? Maybe I can figure out what she's saying. But you need to be calm so you don't frighten her. Or Mimi."

Bri looked sideways at him. How could he be so calm when her baby was—

"Can you do that?"

She nodded jerkily. Sniffed back tears she hadn't been aware of. And somehow they were back at the house.

David dropped his jacket in the mudroom and went straight through the kitchen.

"The door on the right," she told him.

He didn't wait for her but plowed ahead.

And she was grateful.

He was already sitting beside Lily when Bri reached the bedroom. He was talking to her, saying something to Mimi. He felt Lily's forehead, pressed his fingers under her ears and jaw. Talking gently the whole time he poked and prodded.

"What is it?" Bri asked, only vaguely aware that he was doing more than asking Lily what hurt. He was examining her. Like he knew what he was doing. His hands moved to her stomach and he pressed gently. She whimpered. But when he pressed again she let out a wail.

"Okay, Lily." He rattled something off in Mandarin. And said over his shoulder, "It looks like appendicitis. How far is the nearest hospital?"

Bri's tongue cleaved to her mouth. "Ten, fifteen minutes. The hospital?"

"Get your purse, insurance cards, cell phone. Call Nick Prescott and ask him to call ahead and tell them we're coming. That it's a suspected case of acute pediatric appendicitis and we may need emergency surgery. Got that?"

Bri nodded. It was all she could manage. Who was this man?

"Then go warm up the car and come back for Mimi. I'll

bring Lily. Remove her car seat. I'll sit in back with her. Bri, just stay calm. It should be all right."

Should. Should be all right, Bri thought as she gathered her purse, checked her wallet. Got her cell phone and hit speed dial for Nick. *Should be, not would be*. Lily had to be all right. She just had to be.

"Prescott," Nick answered in a groggy voice.

"Nick, it's Bri."

"What's happened?" He was fully awake now. She could hear him moving around.

"Lily's sick. We're taking her to the hospital. David said—" Her voice caught. "David said to tell them we're driving her there and that it's acute appendicitis, pediatric appendicitis, and we may need a surgeon. Oh Nick."

"I'm on it. Here, talk to Margaux."

"I can't. I have to get the car warm. I'll call her later."

"Okay, I'll call the hospital. You go. Be careful. I'll meet you there."

She started to say he didn't have to but he'd already hung up.

When she came back from the car, David was talking to Mimi, who had at least calmed to a whimper. She saw Bri and scampered off the bed. She'd put her slippers on over her pajama feet and was clutching her teddy bear. She was trying to help. Bri's heart was so full of love and fear she thought it might burst. But she managed a smile at Mimi and scooped her up.

Mimi was docile as Bri put her into her snow jacket, all the while murmuring every comforting word she knew in her broken Mandarin. And promised to become proficient if they just made it through this crisis.

Mimi clung to her as she carried her out to the SUV. She began to cry again when Bri strapped her into her car seat and grabbed at her when she tried to close the door. Bri hugged her, kissed her, reassured her, and shut the door. Mimi let out a howl.

David had wrapped Lily in her comforter and he carried his bundle out the door. Bri opened the car door and he climbed in back with his bundle. As he did, something fell to the ground. Bri reached over to pick it up. Lily's scruffy stuffed bunny.

He'd remembered to bring the stuffed animal. Bri picked it up and their eyes met. She handed him the bunny and shut the door.

The ride to the hospital seemed interminable, and Bri had to fight not to floor the accelerator. But the roads were icy in the dark and she was carrying too precious a cargo to fail now. So she kept her eyes on the road, trying to block out Lily's cries and Mimi's responding whimpers.

And Bri began to sing, unaware of what she was doing, and it calmed her and the backseat grew quiet and she prayed and sang until she saw the lights of the hospital.

She stopped the SUV at the emergency room entrance. David got out and carried Lily through the automatic doors. Bri looked around for a place to park, found nothing. She didn't have time to look. She got out, fumbled with Mimi's car seat, lifted her and the stuffed bear out, and rushed inside, only to see David carrying Lily through double stainless steel doors.

"Are you Mrs. Boyce?" A wiry African-American woman in blue scrubs was holding a clipboard. "Dr. Mosley is examining her in room four if you'd like to come with me."

"Yes." But when she got to room four, only David was there.

"They've taken her down for a CT scan." He stepped toward her and put his arms around her and Mimi. "They seem very competent here."

The nurse left, another one took her place. "Are you the parents?"

Bri jumped away. "I'm Brianna Boyce, Lily's mother."

"I see. We'll need you to come fill out the insurance and release forms, please."

"Release forms?" Bri's mind couldn't seem to understand what was going on. She had to pull herself together. They were at the hospital, they were going to take care of Lily. She would be fine. She had to be.

"In order to allow the surgery," the nurse explained patiently.

Bri looked at David.

"They'll need to remove Lily's appendix," he said. "Go sign the papers."

"Yes, of course." She stepped away from him.

"Dr. Henderson, Dr. Mosley asked if you would explain to the patient what is going to happen."

Bri heard David breathe but she didn't turn around.

The nurse was already walking down the corridor, and Bri numbly followed. Had the nurse just called David Doctor?

The first thing she saw when she reached the waiting room was Nick coming through the door.

He saw Bri and hurried toward her. "I moved your car. You left the keys in it. Do you need anything out of it?"

"No. Thank you. You didn't have to come."

"Of course I did. Margaux will be here soon. She's waiting for Jude to come stay with Connor."

Bri burst into tears. Mimi began wailing.

"It'll be fine. But you have to fill out forms. Give Mimi to me."

Mimi only screamed louder when Nick tried to take her. So the three of them went into the business office together.

Bri signed form after form, mindless, without reading them. Just scribbled a semblance of her name as fast as she could. So they could operate on her Lily. It seemed to go on forever.

Once the papers were signed and the insurance cards photocopied, they were told to take the elevator to the third floor where they could wait for the doctor. They'd barely sat down when Dr. Mosley came into the room. He shook hands with Nick and explained what was happening. They were going to remove Lily's appendix. They were going into the operating room immediately. The appendix was intact so far. The sooner the surgery, the easier on the patient it would be.

The doctor left. Bri signed more papers. The nurse left just as Margaux walked into the room.

"I got here as soon as I could. How is she?"

"They're operating now. David went with them," Bri said. "Nick, what did you tell them when you called? When we got here they called him Dr. Henderson."

Nick looked at his wife. Margaux looked at Nick.

"They called him Dr. Henderson because he is a doctor."

Chapter Eight

· · · · · · · · · ·

"A DOCTOR? A real medical doctor?"

Margaux nodded and led Bri and Mimi, who was still clinging to her neck, over to a couch. "Nick, maybe you could go see if you could find us some decent coffee?"

Nick scowled at her, but left the room.

"I don't get it," Bri said. "He's been practically living at my house, I've told him my life story, and he never said a word. He made it sound like his life was schlepping boxes of supplies to refugees." She shifted Mimi in her lap. "And why the hell would a doctor hitchhike across the country?"

"He's been volunteering for the last ten years. I don't think he had the kind of patients who could pay for their care."

"And how come you and Nick know this and I don't?"

"I guess David explained it to Nick while they were talking the other day. He wasn't going to tell me. It was one of those guy things. But I was worried about David staying in your caretaker's cottage. I mean, we really didn't know anything about him.

"Nick ended up telling me parts of it to keep me from coming over to your house and spending the night." She shrugged. "The rest I either guessed or wheedled out of Nick when his attention was on something else."

Bri passed her free hand over her face. "I should be thankful. I just wish I had known. Maybe then I wouldn't have panicked so badly if I knew that he knew what he was doing."

She glanced up at the big round wall clock. It had been over an hour since they'd brought Lily to the hospital. Only ten minutes since the nurse had left with the permission papers. "Do you think she'll be all right?"

Margaux scooted closer and put her arm around Bri, stroked Mimi's hair. "I'm sure . . . I hope so."

Nick was gone nearly fifteen minutes. When he did return he was carrying a big brown bag.

Margaux jumped up to relieve him of the bag. "Where did you have to go to get this?" she asked, pulling out cups, napkins, and plastic-covered pastries.

"I didn't. I called Finley and he dropped by Dottie's for the coffee. And Dottie being Dottie added what she thought you girls might want." Margaux pulled out a thermos.

"It's Finley's. Dottie commandeered it because she didn't want the refills to get cold."

"Well, thank your deputy for all of us. And tell him I'll return his thermos." Margaux handed a cup to Bri.

Bri took it, but simply held it in her hands and looked back at the clock.

MIMI HAD FALLEN asleep at last and was lying on the couch with a hospital blanket over her. Nick and Margaux were talking quietly in the corner. Bri had finally stopped watching the clock and was pacing the floor when Dr. Mosley entered, followed by David, unshaven, wrinkled, and looking like he'd been through the wars.

Bri stopped pacing. Nick and Margaux automatically came to stand by her.

The doctor smiled. "Everything went very well. We were able to remove the appendix laproscopically. If everything goes as it should, you'll have her home for Christmas."

Bri began to shake. "Thank you. Can I see her?"

"Of course. She's still groggy, but she wants to see her mama."

"Oh." Bri jerked forward. Turned back to Mimi.

"We'll stay with Mimi," Margaux said.

Bri could only nod, she was too close to tears of relief, mixed with emotions she couldn't begin to name. Joy, confusion, hope, and, strangely enough, anger. She headed blindly to the door, passing David without a word.

DAVID DIDN'T EVEN watch her go. He felt numb. Sick. It had been years since he'd been in a real hospital, and yet it all came back to him in one blinding moment when he carried that little girl through the emergency room doors.

It was all so familiar, almost like he'd never left. And yet so much had changed within him since then. The admission procedure, the smell of the corridors, the white coats, the colorful scrubs. The things you didn't have in the field, where surgeries were done in Quonset huts if you were lucky, in a tent or worse if you weren't.

Here, everything was so clean. He'd forgotten how clean it was.

Margaux nudged him with a cup of coffee. He took it. Walked over to one of the prefabricated chairs and sat down, holding the cup in both hands. Felt a hand on his arm.

Margaux Prescott was looking down at him, concern in her eyes. "Are you okay? Hungry? Dottie from the diner sent over pastries, though you might want something more substantial after the night you've had."

"No thanks."

"We're all so grateful to you."

He shook his head.

"Bri knows you're a doctor. Does it matter?"

"Was."

"Whatever. She heard the nurse call you 'doctor' and wondered why. I told her because you were one."

"It's okay. Thanks for the coffee." She left him alone after that, but he knew they were both watching him. They must think it weird that he denied his ability. His avocation. Hiding his light under a bushel, his missionary father would say. But that light had gone out months ago, had been diminishing steadily with each epidemic, malnourished child, blind old man, or barely recognizable body that still lived. A shudder went through him and coffee splashed to the floor. He rubbed it dry with his boot.

The room was still. Someone had turned the volume off in the old television that flickered from a wall shelf, like old televisions in waiting rooms everywhere, everywhere but in the field. The only sound was the maddening ticking of the institutional clock. And the thump and jump of his own heart.

He stood, put his cup in the trash. "I think I'll go see if Bri needs anything, and then if you could ask someone to drop me off at her house."

"Sure," Margaux said. "She'll need some clothes, at least. Knowing Bri, she'll stay here for the duration. I'll drop you off and take Mimi home with me, then come back for you. Connor can stay home from school today and entertain her. You're welcome to come, too."

BRI SAT CLOSE to the hospital bed, holding Lily's tiny hand. The rambunctious, chubby-cheeked girl looked so small and fragile. Her black hair, spread across the white pillow, haloed a face so pale that fear raced up Bri's spine.

An IV that the nurse said was antibiotics ran from her little arm. Her stuffed rabbit sat on the bedside table where she'd be able to see it when she woke up.

She was so still. Bri wished she'd move or something,

but knew she was sedated. She took in a long breath, eased it out.

What if David hadn't been there? What if she'd been alone and waited until the morning to see if Lily were better? What if she'd waited too late? Lily could have died.

Her eyes filled with tears. Maybe she didn't deserve these beautiful children after all. She'd wanted to do some good in the world, but maybe she wasn't up to it. Maybe the world didn't want her to be useful, caring, happy. Maybe she was a fool to think that she could do it alone.

"How is she?"

Bri turned her head, blinking furiously. David stood several feet away, as if he didn't want to get too close to them. "She looks so . . . so little." Her voice cracked.

He smiled, but it was a tired smile. "She is little. But she'll be fine. Margaux said she'd bring you whatever you needed."

Bri looked down at her pajamas, realizing for the first time she wasn't fully clothed. Her mouth twisted and the tears fell against her control.

David took two steps and pulled her up. Wrapped his arms around her and held her close while she tried not to cry. She cried anyway. And felt a little better afterward.

She pushed him away, not roughly but so she could see his face, the model in her raising her head long enough to realize her own face must looked blotched and hideous.

She meant to thank him for all he'd done. For going the extra mile when it was obvious all he wanted to do was deliver his letter and leave. But what she said was, "Why didn't you tell me you were a doctor?"

"It didn't come up."

"Something that big? And it just didn't come up? Why didn't you want us to know? Or was it just me?"

"Don't be ridiculous. I'm not a doctor now. So it seemed superfluous."

"What if you hadn't been there? What if I hadn't called you to talk to Lily? What if you'd left that first day?" She was talking to herself as much as David, questioning her ability to raise these girls she loved so much. She was wound so tight and so close to the edge of something that might turn into hysteria. She heard herself and couldn't stop.

"What if I'd never come?" He smiled at her. "You would have taken her to the hospital just like you did this morning. You'd be sitting here waiting for her to wake up or in the waiting room with Mimi and the Prescotts. Just like now."

"How do you know? She might have died. Maybe I was crazy to think I could do this."

He grasped her shoulders, shook her. "Stop it. You're just a little post-traumatic right now. Lily is fine. You'll learn as you go, just like every mother before you. And you have a terrific support system. You'll be fine."

She covered her face with her hands. "I just don't want to screw up again."

"You didn't screw up. You just happened to have help. You really didn't need me. I saw you in action. You didn't need me at all."

Something in his voice made her forget about her fears and her feelings of inadequacy. "Who are you trying to convince, David. Me or you?"

"Just tell me what you want Margaux to bring you from home."

She didn't press him, but wrote out a list and handed it to him. He stuck it his pocket and walked to the door.

"David?"

He turned. "Hmmm?"

"Why did you quit practicing medicine?"

He shrugged slightly. "Because it didn't change one damn thing." He turned and was gone, leaving Bri to stare at the empty doorway.

Chapter Nine

·········

MARGAUX STOPPED HER car at Bri's kitchen door. They hadn't talked much on the drive from the hospital, for which David was grateful. He was suddenly exhausted. He practically crawled out of the car.

"Thanks for the ride."

"No problem."

He started walking toward the cottage.

"Hang on for a sec." She pulled out the list and scribbled something at the end. Then she tore it off and handed it to him. "My cell number. Call when you want a ride back to the hospital, or if you want to come over for dinner or something. Do you have food? Should I go get you some lunch?

"No, but thanks."

"I'm sorry I let the cat out of the bag about you being a doctor."

"It's no big deal. Doesn't matter in the least."

"She heard them call you doctor at the hospital. She had a right to know."

"It's fine, Margaux. Don't give it another thought." He didn't wait, but strode away before she could call him back again.

As soon as he was inside the cottage, he tossed off his jacket, took a long hard look at his backpack where it still lay on the floor. Stay or leave? Life would have been so much simpler if he had just dropped Ben's letter in a mailbox. Now he could feel those pernicious strings of caring tying him to the spot. How could he leave until Lily was totally recovered? How would Bri manage?

Just like she managed before you stumbled into her life, fool. She didn't need him, those kids didn't need him. The truth was, nobody needed him. He thought he would like it here but he didn't. Blame it on his missionary parents, his decision to become a doctor. To go where he was needed, not where he could settle down in a nice town to a comfortable practice.

He sat on the edge of the bed and untied his boots, kicked them off. Lay down and pulled the blanket over him. He had done some good. But it hadn't lasted. What was the point of saving a village from disease just to have it raided by an opposing tribe and the people killed a few months later? Why set up triage centers when they were blown to smithereens before the fist patient could be seen?

What the hell was the point?

He fell asleep on the question.

David awoke a couple of hours later, feeling somewhat

refreshed and immensely hungry. He wondered if Margaux had locked Bri's door.

Mercifully, the back door to the farmhouse was unlocked. He rummaged in the fridge, careful not to eat anything they might need. Then he read the note Margaux had left tented on the kitchen table. *I mean it, call me if you need anything.* Again she'd left her cell number. This time she'd added Nick's cell and their landline.

David shook his head. They were all bending over backwards to make him feel welcome. And it was the last thing in the world he wanted. He wanted to be alone, unattached, detached, uncaring. To be any other way was just too damn hard.

He made himself an egg sandwich and then went outside, where he chopped wood until his arms and back ached. He replenished the wood pile, then looked around for something else that needed doing.

The phone numbers sitting on the table kept beckoning. He wanted to know how Lily was doing. If Mimi was okay without her Mama Boy. Finally he gave it up, showered, changed into the last of his clean clothes, and started walking toward the hospital.

He hopped a ride in the back of a pickup truck that let him off a block away from the hospital. He stopped at the gift shop, and bought a helium balloon with a big yellow smiley face and *Get Well Soon* written across it, then he took the elevator to the third floor.

It was with a mixture of anticipation and trepidation that he opened the door to Lily's room. He checked on the threshold. The woman sitting in the chair next to Lily's bed was not Bri. For the briefest second he thought it was Margaux, but when she turned to see who had entered, he knew he had to be looking at Margaux's mother. What was her name? Jude.

"You must be David," she said, breaking into a smile.

Why were they all so ready to be nice to him?

"I'm Jude Sullivan, Margaux's mother."

"Nice to meet you. I just—" He looked up at the balloon.

"Well, come on in. Lily, look what Dr. Henderson brought you."

"Day-did," Lily said sleepily. "Boon."

Jude beamed at Lily. "That's right, he's brought you a balloon." She motioned for David to come closer.

David stepped toward the bed.

"Mama gone."

Jude leaned over and patted her hand. "Mama's gone to see Mimi. She's coming back soon."

Lily looked at David.

"She'll be back soon."

She asked again in Mandarin.

"Back soon," David repeated.

Lily nodded. "Back soo. Back soo. Back soo." Her eyes closed.

David sighed and tied the balloon to the dresser across the room where Lily could see it.

"I think the saints must have brought you to us, David Henderson."

"I'm afraid the saints gave up on me a long time ago, Mrs. Sullivan."

"Hmmph. Call me Jude. Everyone else does. The saints never give up on a person. Maybe you've given up on yourself?"

David had been smiling at her, but her statement wiped the expression off his face.

"Have I offended you? Sorry. But I sense a man about to bolt. Stay awhile and give us a chance to thank you properly."

"I didn't do anything but make the mistake of sleeping in the wrong barn."

"Do you really think it was a mistake?"

"Well, it wasn't ordained, if that's what you're thinking." He heard the bitterness in his voice. Started to apologize for his rudeness.

Jude laughed, a melodious sound that disarmed him. And confused him.

"I'm not *that* religious. I'm sure everyone's life would have gone on perfectly well, whether you entered it or not. But you've certainly enriched it."

"I see where Margaux gets her tenacity."

Jude smiled complacently. "I taught her well. We've all had our ups and downs. That's the beauty of family and friends. They give you a soft place to land. Now if you don't mind sitting here for a minute, I'll go get myself a cup of tea. Would you care for anything?"

Taken off guard, David could only shake his head and sit down.

BRI SAT ON Margaux's couch sipping tea and holding Mimi on her lap. Mimi had cried when Bri came in from the hospital. Bri just picked her up and held her. How could she ever make her tiny daughter understand that she would never leave her, if she had her way? And she wasn't looking forward to leaving her to go back to the hospital.

"Was I crazy to think I could do this by myself?"

Margaux frowned at her. "Of course not. Anyway, you're not by yourself."

"It was just a fluke that David —Dr. Henderson—showed up out of the blue, like some flaming miracle."

"I wasn't talking about David."

Bri sighed. "I know. I'm sorry. I know I have you and Nick and Jude and Dottie and Grace . . . okay, a whole lot of people. It's just him showing up, speaking Chinese, and diagnosing appendicitis that showed me how incompetent I am."

"Bullshit. If his coming has shown you anything, it's that maybe you're in need of a little companionship."

Bri laughed in spite of herself. "You make me sound like an old woman with a hundred cats."

Margaux laughed, too. "I did not. I just think he's ruffled your peace." She cocked her head at Bri.

"Oh no. Not going there. You know what happens with me and men. I have responsibilities now."

"I know what *happened* with you and men. Happened, past tense. That was ages ago. Exactly when was the last time you had any dealings with men?"

"Jake McGuire redid my banister and several treads this fall."

"And don't think Nick and I didn't notice."

"He's sweet but a little too good-natured for me."

Margaux chuckled.

"What?"

"At least you thought about it."

Bri sighed.

"Look, it's hard to suddenly have kids already walking around and going to school, without having time to wrap your mind around it and waiting for them to learn to talk and walk and all those things that most mother's have months to prepare for. Dealing with Connor is often beyond my expertise, and as for Nick, fuggedaboutit. That's why we have grandparents."

"My parents came to visit a few weeks ago," Bri said. "They lasted a day. It was too stressful for everyone. They did invite us to go there for Christmas, but I wanted the girls to have Christmas in their own home."

"Absolutely. Plus we wanted you all to be here with us. And they have mom and Nick's mom to spoil them." Margaux smiled happily. "It's our first Christmas together, too. Which reminds me. Are you all set for . . ." She glanced at Mimi. "S-A-N-T-A?"

"Yes, thank goodness. I've been buying stuff for months now. I probably shouldn't give it all to them at once. Talk about overkill."

"Us, too. Trying to make up for all the bad stuff they've been through, Connor, and Lily and Mimi."

Mimi looked up at the sound of her name. "Mimi," she said.

"I should get back to the hospital," Bri said. "Dr. Mosley said that Lily might be able to come home for Christmas Eve. That's tomorrow. I really, really hope that happens. Do you think they would let Mimi in to see Lily if I took her with me?"

"See Lily," Mimi said.

Margaux smiled at Bri. "We'll all go."

Chapter Ten

· · · · · · · · · ·

"SHE'S BEEN TALKING a mile a minute," the nurse said as she wheeled Lily out into the late afternoon sun. She stopped the chair next to the SUV and lifted her into her car seat. "Couldn't understand most of what she said but she's won our hearts."

"Bye bye." The nurse flapped her fingers at Lily.

"Bye-bye," Lily said and waggled her hand.

The nurse smiled past Lily to Mimi. "Bye bye."

"Thanks for everything," Bri told her, and closed the car door.

"Merry Christmas," the nurse said, and pushed the empty wheelchair away.

Bri drove back home, both girls in the backseat, only instead of an empty passenger seat, David Henderson sat beside her. It was a strange feeling, and not an image she wanted to get used to. He'd been a tremendous help just at a time when she really needed help. She even got a little buzz when he was around. But neither of them would act on it. He was carrying way too much baggage, whatever it was, and she was too distrustful of men and herself to mess up now.

When they got home, Bri settled Lily on the couch in the great room. At least she tried to. One look at the presents under the tree and Lily would not stay down.

"If you both sit quietly on the couch, you can each open one present tonight."

David laughed. "You think you can stop them at one?"

"We were always allowed to open one package on Christmas Eve." She smiled a reminiscent smile. "But nothing big."

She picked out two identical packages for Lily and Mimi to open. At first both girls just looked at them.

"Open them," Bri said. "Mimi and Lily's presents." Their expressions changed and they tore through the paper to reveal identical boxes filled with colorful hair bands, barrettes, and ribbons. Their expressions of happy surprise made Bri's lip tremble.

"I better put the lasagna in the oven." Leaving David to keep things in check, she fled the room. She was so overful of emotion she couldn't contain it. But she didn't want the girls—or David, for that matter—to see her cry. She wasn't sure she could explain "happy tears."

A couple of deep breaths and the sight of the waiting lasagna calmed her. She still wasn't the best cook in the world but wanted to make the Boyce traditional Christmas Eve dinner for her girls, and after a few tips from David and a couple of emergency calls to her mother, it looked perfect.

She spread a red tablecloth on the kitchen table and placed a snowman made from Styrofoam balls in the center. She grinned at her handiwork. Life was looking up.

When she came back to the great room, David was sitting on the couch. Mimi and Lily had headfuls of colorful barrettes and banded cowlicks that passed for ponytails. They knelt on the couch on either side of David.

"Hey, here's Mama Boy," he said.

Bri looked down at him. She covered her mouth with her hand but couldn't keep back the laugh. "Nice hair."

David grinned. His hair was spiked in a handful of little cowlicks held by the girls' new hair bands and barrettes.

"We did," Lily informed her. Mimi nodded.

"Lovely," Bri said.

"I think I'll go primp for dinner," David said. He wriggled out from between the girls and headed for the back door, pulling out the hair bands on his way.

"Dinner in an hour," Bri called after him. Laughing, she chose a book and sat down. Mimi and Lily climbed into her lap. "Let's see." She opened it to the first page. "'Twas the night before . . .'"

WHEN DAVID RETURNED an hour later he wore clean clothes and his hair was still damp from the shower.

"Lasagna smells incredible," he said.

"Well keep your fingers crossed. It's the first time I've made it."

By the time dinner was over the girls were fading and so

was Bri, but there was Santa still to do. She put them to bed. They could have baths tomorrow before they went to Margaux and Nick's for Christmas lunch.

When she got back to the great room, David had poured out two glasses of wine.

"Thought you might need some fortification and some help lugging stuff down the chimney. Are they asleep?"

"Out like little lights."

They crept upstairs to the spare room where more packages waited. They were all wrapped in candy-cane-striped paper.

"The official paper of the North Pole," Bri told him.

They lugged the presents downstairs, arranged them around the tree, and sat down.

"Pretty nice," David said. "Thanks for letting me be a part of it."

"Hey, you've more than earned your keep."

He smiled.

"Why don't you practice medicine anymore?"

The smile vanished. "I just don't."

"But—"

"I told you at the hospital, Bri. I burned out. There are just too many sick and maimed people in the world, too much inhumanity. Too much red tape and uncaring and greedy officials. It was just too big of a job."

"You said at the hospital that it didn't change things, but you must have helped people, saved their lives."

"Yeah, just so they could succumb to something else, another disease, or by violence. I lost a lot that should have been saved because we didn't have the right medicines or the right equipment or even a Jeep to take them to a decent hospital. I saved others that it would have been better to let die.

"It's a god-awful world out there, Bri. I'm glad you helped Mimi and Lily find their way out of it."

"You could practice here . . . or somewhere like here. You'd have the equipment and the facilities. You could help people here."

"No. I don't have it in me anymore. And that's that."

"Take a break. Do something else for a while. But you can't just stop being a doctor. You can't unlearn what you know."

"I can try."

They fell into silence. Bri wanted to shake him. He just possibly had saved Lily's life. It just seemed wrong for him to quit like that. He hadn't lost a hand or an eye, nothing was preventing him from going back to medicine. She didn't get it. But she knew better than to push it further.

"Well, thank you for bringing Ben's letter to Nick; whatever it said sure seemed to help. I know he's felt responsible for Ben's death." *Sort of like you, responsible for them all,* she wanted to say, but she didn't.

"It seemed like the right thing to do . . . Bri?"

"Yes?"

"You have a really nice family. Just go with your gut and everything will be fine."

She frowned at him. "Oh . . . kay."

He drained his glass. "I'd better get going."

"Sure," Bri said. "I know the girls will be up at the break of day to see what Santa has left them."

"In addition to all the other gifts." His eyes were teasing, and a little sad, Bri thought.

"I know I got a little carried away, but I've been shopping for over a year now in anticipation of this. They came with only those two ratty stuffed animals I took with me to China."

"I wasn't making a judgment." He swallowed. "They're very lucky girls."

"Thanks," Bri said. "I really appreciate all your—"

He put his fingers over her lips, stopping her. "They're very lucky. Good night."

He gave her one last long and unreadable look. She followed him out to the mudroom, waited while he put on boots and coat.

"Set your alarm," she said. "You don't want to miss all the fun."

He smiled and walked out the door.

She watched from the window as he crossed the snow toward the cottage, his body silhouetted by the moon. He was halfway across the field when he turned and seemed to look straight at her. She slipped into the obscurity of the shadows. She didn't want to be caught watching him.

DAVID TOOK A last long look at the farmhouse. He wanted to remember it. Not that he would likely forget it or its occupants. He knew he would have no choice but to remember it, and he wanted to get it right. He should have never stayed so long, let himself get involved with this family, made friends with Bri's friends. Met Ben Prescott's brother and his son. Nick's wife. Margaux's mother.

His soul, what was left of it, was restless. If he stayed still too long, the weight of his past, all that he'd not been able to do, would begin to suffocate him. It was only a matter of time until it did that here. And then everyone would be disappointed, and hurt, and his selfishness would be the cause.

No, as much as he hated not seeing the faces of those two little girls in the morning experiencing their first Christmas, he knew the right thing to do.

He wrote a quick note, which he left on the little worktable next to a clumsily wrapped present. They'd be disappointed at first, but not as disappointed as they would be if he stayed.

He pushed his clothes into his backpack, but tonight he didn't drop it on the floor. Tonight he slung it over his shoulders and went out the cottage door. The lights in the farmhouse were already turned out.

He began walking across the moonlit snow; he didn't look back at the house again, but headed for the road.

Chapter Eleven

· · · · · · · · · ·

BRI WOKE UP to sunlight. A glance at the clock said it was eight o'clock. Surely the girls had awakened earlier to see what Santa had brought. She was sure they understood about Santa.

Maybe David had taken them in the kitchen to let her sleep for a while longer. That would be just like him. Bri showered quickly and dressed in jeans and a Christmas sweater with jingle bells that she'd found in a thrift store. She slipped on her Uggs and hurried out to get things rolling.

It was totally quiet. There was no smell of coffee. She backtracked to the girls' bedroom and peaked in. They were both still asleep. Crazy. In the Boyce household, they were all up at five and badgering their parents to get up so they could open their presents.

She went into the kitchen. No David. She made coffee

and while it was brewing, shrugged into her jacket and ran across the field to wake him.

She knocked on the door. Jumped on the balls of her feet trying to keep warm. "David. No slouching today. It's Christmas. Merry Christmas."

She knocked again.

"David?" She opened the door and stepped inside. Listened for the sound of the shower. But there was only quiet. The quiet of emptiness. She went toward the bedroom but stopped when she saw the notepaper propped against a round package. And she was overcome with a chill that started in her gut and spread to fill her body and her heart.

He was gone. She bypassed the note and went into the bedroom. No David, no coat, no backpack. He'd left a note. A damned note.

She went back to the table, snatched the note up and read through a blur of tears she refused to let fall. He didn't deserve her tears. The jackass. He didn't even bother to say goodbye.

What was she going to tell the girls? Margaux and Nick were expecting him for lunch. Everybody was waiting to meet him. And he was gone.

"You could have waited until after lunch, you jerk!"

She snapped the note in the air. Dashed away the blur in her eyes. Read it again. *I'm sorry. I knew I wouldn't be able to say goodbye so I took the coward's way out.* "I'll say." Bri sniffed. *Tell the girls goodbye and I'll miss them.* "The hell I will. You can go to hell. I'll tell the girls you went to hell."

She crumpled up the note, then spread it out again on

the table and folded it. Margaux would want to see it for herself.

Bri sank into the chair next to the table. She knew she should go back to the house, wake the girls, try to make their first Christmas together the best day in the whole world. But she couldn't get past her anger at David.

"HE'S NOT COMING," Bri told Margaux as the girls ran past her into the kitchen.

"Why? Is he afraid he'll be out of place? He won't be."

"No. It's because he's gone." Bri stopped in the mudroom to take off her Uggs and change into flats.

"Gone where?"

"Wherever the road takes him," Bri said in sepulchral tones. "I guess. He didn't say. Just walked out of the house last night and that's the last we saw of him. The girls think he was Santa Claus, because Connor told them no one can ever see Santa leave presents. Though how they understand Connor is beyond me."

"Kids," Margaux said, and led her into the warm kitchen. "So did you try to explain to them?"

"No. I couldn't use words to describe him that would be appropriate in front of children. He left them a present . . . in the cottage for me to find. With a note." Bri reached into her purse and pulled it out. "Figured you'd want to see it."

"I'll say." Margaux took the note, unfolded it and frowned at it. "Holy cow. The man has issues."

"Mags, we all have issues. We don't run away ."

"Who's run away?" asked Jude, coming into the kitchen. "Merry Christmas, Bri." She kissed Bri on the cheek. "Where's David?"

Bri rolled her eyes. Margaux handed Jude the note.

"Oh dear," Jude said, and handed the note back to Bri. "I was hoping that wouldn't happen."

Bri broke. "Of all the times to leave. How selfish could he be? He couldn't wait one more day? He could have left two days ago, before the girls became so attached to him. It's just cruel."

"I think it was more self-protective than wanting to be cruel."

"Yeah, well I've learned my lesson . . . again." She turned to Margaux. "See, I told you. This is why I stay away from men. They screw everything up."

The kitchen door opened. Nick came in. "I'm ready to carve the bird. We're all salivating out there." He looked around. "Where's David?"

Margaux handed him the carving knife. "Don't ask."

"Gone," echoed Bri.

"Oh."

Jude opened a package of rolls and put them on a cookie sheet. "Do me a favor, Bri. Don't give up on him. I think he'll be back."

"I don't think so."

"Oh maybe not today, but someday. I think he knew he could have a life here and it scared him."

Bri groaned. "That's so much bunk. Look at this group.

There's not one scary person in it. Not even Nick . . . any-more." She smiled, and it was the first time that day smiling hadn't been an effort.

"Thank you very much," Nick said. "I know his timing was lousy. But being a guy, I know that it's sometimes hard to do the right thing at the right time. No matter how hard you try you're bound to screw something up."

Margaux laughed and put her arms around his neck. "Thanks for that insight into male behavior, Chief. I'll try to remember it. Now would you please carve that turkey before it dries out?"

Jude handed Bri a casserole dish, and Bri carried it into the dining room, stopping by the parlor to say a quick Merry Christmas to the crowd, who were laughing and talking as they waited for lunch. It was like a giant extended family. Grace, who was Bri and Margaux's best friend since child-hood, came over to stand on tiptoe and give her a big hug and a questioning look.

"Gone like the summer," Bri told her. "Tell you later."

Soon the table was covered in serving dishes. What there was no room for spilled over to the sideboard.

"Sit down everyone," Margaux said. "Let's get this show on the road."

There was a moment of silence while Connor said the blessing followed by Mimi's "Ah-min" and Lily's louder "Ah-choo." There was stifled laughter around the table. Bri poked her and she said sweetly, "Ah-min."

"Dig in," said Margaux. And they did. Dishes were passed

and conversations bounced around the table. Bri filled plates for herself and Mimi and Lily though they looked questioningly at the asparagus casserole and the crescent rolls.

The room slipped from near rowdiness into silence and sighs as the first bites were taken.

"Delicious," said Roger Kyle, Jude's new husband.

"Thank you," said Margaux. "It was a group effort."

There was a noise from the kitchen.

"Was that the door?" Margaux asked.

"Wind must have shut it." Nick stood up. "I'll see."

"Can you pass the gravy?" asked Jude. "I've been living on poached eggs for a week just for gravy."

Everyone laughed.

Nick stepped back into the room. He wasn't alone. David Henderson stood next to him, looking a little embarrassed and seriously uncomfortable.

Bri's mouth dropped open.

"Day-did," cried Lily, and slid off her chair to run to him.

"Careful sport," he said.

Mimi was right behind her. "Day-did," she echoed, and threw her arms around his legs.

The room was suddenly silent. Jude jumped up. "So glad you could make it after all. Here, let me make you a plate. We saved you a seat."

David glanced at Bri, but she looked away and began talking to Grace on her far side.

Wow, Grace mouthed, and pretended to listen.

David shepherded the girls back to their seats. Bri ignored

him. She wasn't sure she could trust herself to say anything nice.

He sat down next to Jude and the meal went on.

After dessert the men turned on the football game and the kids went up to Connor's room to play with his new toys.

Bri started to go with them to keep an eye on the convalescing Lily.

"Take a break, " Grace said. "This is what honorary aunties are for." She climbed the stairs after them.

Bri joined Margaux and Jude in the kitchen.

"Some things never change," said Jude. "Every Christmas, the men end up in front of the television and the women end up in the kitchen. So much for women's lib." She chuckled. "And I wouldn't have it any other way. You girls load the dishwasher. I'll wash the glasses."

A few minutes later Nick and David came into the kitchen.

"I came to apologize," David said.

The three women turned around.

"Should we leave?" Jude asked.

"No," David said. "To all of you. For walking out without saying goodbye. But especially to Bri, who showed me kindness and who deserved better."

Bri blinked hard.

"I thought I needed to go before I got too attached to everyone in Crescent Cove. Since I've been here, I started to feel like I might actually be able to start a new life here. I'd find myself thinking about finding a job, or even sometimes I could see myself opening a practice, and then I'd think about all the people who needed help, who needed doctors and didn't have them, and how Crescent Cove certainly didn't need one more crowding the others. And I felt like I was . . . I don't know, betraying them or . . ." He shrugged. Obviously he was having a hard time articulating what he felt.

"So what made you decide to come back?" asked Bri.

"I was standing out on I-95, about five miles from Stamford, freezing my—freezing and wondering where I was going and why the hell I couldn't just accept the fact that I liked it here. I liked the people here. That I really could have a life here. Maybe not as a doctor but as something. And I thought about how long it would take to walk to the next town and the town after that. And if I kept going, would I ever be able to stop?

"And suddenly I realized that I was a damn fool if I didn't turn around and accept what I could have here. At least give it a try."

He shrugged. "So I crossed to the other side of the interstate and hitched a ride back again." He looked at Bri. "Is the cottage still available?"

She fought the smile that was stretching at her lips. And gave up the battle. "Yes. But so help me, don't you ever do that again." She glared at him. "And by the way, the girls think you're Santa Claus."

"You didn't tell them that?"

"Of course not, it was Connor. Actually I think it was Lily."

Jude linked her arm through David's. "See, things are beginning to work out already."

"I'm not sure I follow you," David said, looking wary.

She squeezed his arm. "Well, being Santa, you'll never have trouble getting a job."

BRI AND DAVID didn't talk much as they drove back to the farmhouse. The girls were pretty quiet. She dropped him up off at the cottage, so he wouldn't have to carry his backpack through the snow.

"I don't want to bother you," Bri said. "But you're welcome at the house anytime, your call."

"Thanks. If you feel uncomfortable with me here..."

"I'll get over it. But next time don't cut out without letting us know."

"I won't. I don't know that I can stay, but I won't do anything rash."

"I can live with that. And no leaving without telling everyone else. I don't want to have to explain to them what I don't understand."

"Fair enough." He got out of the car and she backed up and drove over to her house. He went inside.

The first thing he saw was his present. She hadn't taken it to the girls. Hadn't even opened it to see what it was.

He unpacked. This time he put his clothes in the little closet and his shaving kit in the bathroom. He stored his backpack in the back of the closet. It didn't feel odd. He didn't panic. It felt okay.

He sat down at the table. Looked at the lopsided gift that he'd found in an antique store downtown while Lily was in the hospital. He'd meant to take it with him when he left, something to remember them by. But it was heavy, and besides, he doubted if he ever could forget them, so he'd torn out several pages from a magazine and wrapped it up. For the girls, for Mama Boy.

He smiled, though his chest felt tight. He put on his coat, pushed the package into his coat pocket, and set out across the snow.

The girls were on the floor playing with their new gifts. Bri was stretched out on the couch sound asleep, until the girls saw him and raced across the room, screeching "Daydid, Day-did." Bri stirred. Sat up.

"Sorry," he said. "I brought one more present."

The girls jumped up and down.

"They know *that* word for sure," said Bri, and eased her feet to the floor.

"Go sit by Mama Boy," he told them.

They pattered back to the couch and climbed up beside Bri.

David put the package in her lap. Then he sat on the floor in front of them.

Bri looked at him, then opened the wrapping and brought out a round ball with a little white farmhouse in the center.

"A snow globe," she said. "Look girls, it's a snow globe."

Mimi and Lily leaned over it. Patted it. Looked at Bri.

"You turn it upside down like this. And it snows."

"Lily house," Lily said.

"Mimi house," said Mimi. "Mama house."

"Yes," Bri said, her voice suddenly tight. "Our house." She looked down at David. "Thank you."

"Day-did house?" Mimi asked, peering into the ball.

"Day-did house," squealed Lily and stretched over the back of the couch to point out the window to the little cottage across the field.

Bri looked at David.

"Day-did's house," he agreed. And he meant it.

See where it all began in

Beach Colors

Connecticut

· · · · · · · · · ·

July 199–

THE PORCH STEPS were hot. Margaux Sullivan hopped from one foot to the other while she searched the beach for her friends.

It was the last day of summer. Sunlight floated on the water like a million diamonds. Lazy pinwheels of white filled the sky. Across the Sound, Long Island stretched like a green thread on the horizon. It felt like time would last forever. But tomorrow the houses would be closed up, and the Selkies would be separated for another winter.

Margaux's stomach clenched. This year would be differ-ent. Margaux and Grace were both returning to Hartford with their families, but Brianna was moving to New York. They might never all meet here again.

Stupid. Of course we will. The Selkies will always have each other.

She shielded her eyes against the sun and found the others standing at the water's edge. Brianna posed for the lifeguard, pretending to ignore him, while he practically fell off his seat to get a better look. Grace stood in the water trying not to giggle.

The lifeguard was tall, dark, and handsome, but Bri's mother told her not to fraternize with him because he was a townie. Bri didn't listen.

Margaux had her own tall, dark, and handsome young townie. Well, he wasn't really hers. He was much older and they'd never even spoken. But they had sat across the same table at the library every summer since she was ten—him frowning over his books—her copying dresses from the latest fashion magazines. It was almost like a date. Only he wasn't there this summer, and now she was sorry that she'd never asked him what he was studying.

The screen door slammed behind her and her brother, Danny, ran past her and jumped down to the sand.

"Hey, Magsy. Want a ride to the library?"

"No thanks. I'm busy. And it's Margaux."

Danny grinned back at her. He pushed his motorcycle helmet over unruly red curls and made a bow. "Madame Ma-a-argaux." Then he reached up and scrubbed her hair. "Magsy." The pencil stub that was pushed through her equally unruly curls fell to the steps.

She slapped at his hand but he dodged away. "See ya, Mags." He ran around the side of the house. A minute later she heard his new Honda 500 roar to life. Margaux pulled at her hair. It had taken her ten minutes to get it to lie flat, and now it was every which way again. She picked up the pencil and shoved it behind her ear.

Brothers could be so annoying. She put two fingers to her lips and whistled. Brianna and Grace looked up and started walking toward her. They met halfway and turned as one toward the jetty at the end of the crescent beach.

Brianna led the way, walking ahead as if she were already leaving them. They climbed up the rocks of the jetty, barely paying attention, they had climbed them so often. Then down again to the cove. The tide was in and they had to splash through the water to reach the path that led through the woods.

Margaux lagged behind. Things were changing and she wasn't sure she was ready. She knew some people outgrew the beach, but not the Selkies. Even when they got too old to explore and write secret messages and go crabbing—Margaux would never be too old to go crabbing—the beach would still be a part of them. Would live in a special place inside each of them.

She felt a flutter of nerves. Today they were leaving something of themselves behind—just in case.

It was cooler beneath the pines and scrub oak. Silently they walked along the narrow path, nearly grown over with rhododendron and fern.

When the path veered off, they ducked under the gnarled

tree limb, climbed over the rotten log, and stopped at the entrance of the Grotto. They had discovered it that first summer, an outcropping of rocks and a ledge of granite that formed a shallow cavern. It became their secret hideout where first they made magic potions, or hid from pirates, and later, talked about boys. They had grown older; the sapling whose roots spread over the rock had become a tree.

But the Grotto never changed. It was a magical place that could make dreams come true.

Brianna flipped on her flashlight, crouched down, and ducked beneath the ledge. One by one, each took her place, sitting cross-legged in a circle, knees touching, while the flashlight cast their shadows eerily against the rough stone.

Brianna reached into her string bag and pulled out a Tupperware container. She placed it in the center of the circle, lifted off the top, and glancing at the others, slowly reached back into the bag and pulled out the pink plastic diary where, that morning, each had made her last secret entry. Solemnly, she placed it in the Tupperware container. She closed the lid and sealed it tight.

They gathered around the fissure in the rock wall. Brianna shoved the box inside, and they covered the opening with three large smooth stones.

"The Selkies forever," Brianna intoned in her throaty voice. They crossed their hearts, licked three fingers, and raised them in the air.

"The Selkies forever."

NICK PRESCOTT STOOD on the dark rocks of the jetty, careful not to get his new uniform wet or scuff the polish of his new boots. Tomorrow he would be in Fort Dix, New Jersey. Private Nick Prescott.

For the past two years, he had watched his friends get on with their lives while he stayed behind. The money he'd saved for college dwindled away while he tried to take care of his mother and brother. But now it was his turn.

He would miss the shore. Even though his family only owned a cape in town, he was proud to have grown up here. He wished he could say the same for his brother, Ben.

He was down there now at his lifeguard post, flirting with the blonde. He just didn't get that they would never accept him. No matter how many times Nick told him. They were summer people. But Ben wouldn't listen.

Nick watched the girls join another girl. His heart tightened—just a little—when he saw her halo of red curls. She had been his talisman ever since the summer after his father died. Then she was just a kid, sharing his table at the library. Drawing pictures with the tip of her tongue pressed to the corner of her mouth as she concentrated. Pushing curls out of her face with an impatient hand. He could hardly wait until school was out and she came back to sit across from him.

Only this summer was different. She had grown up, become one of them, and that put an end to everything.

He would become a history professor someday. The army would pay for his education. And she would become—he didn't know. He just knew that she would always be a summer person, and he, just a townie.

Chapter One

• • • • • • • •

MARGAUX SULLIVAN STOOD unmoving and listened to the echoes of her failure. Only a week ago, her Manhattan loft had been thrumming with energy, excitement, and caffeine, as twenty-five pattern cutters, drapers, and seamstresses worked round the clock to prepare M Atelier's latest collection for the event of the year. New York City's Fashion Week.

Now it was just an empty space. The finished pieces carted away in cardboard boxes. The long worktables cleared of everything but a few forgotten scraps of fabric. The mannequins repossessed, the brick walls bare except for the row of five-by-three-foot photographs of Margaux's award-winning fashions that her creditors left behind.

The asymmetrical black moiré satin sheath had been her first CFDA award winner. The black wool tuxedo had made the cover of Vogue. Marie Claire had called the black tulle ball gown—not a fluffy evening dress, but cutting-edge stark—"Tulle with a Bite."

The models stared back at her, caught in time, sleek and scowling. This dress will make you thin, this will make you beautiful, this will make men adore you. Black, unique, and powerful. They'd promised to make Margaux's dream come true.

And it had come true. Ever since that sticky summer day when she'd discovered a bridal magazine in the Crescent Cove library. She'd opened its shiny pages to brilliant white, palest pink, creamy ivory. Pearls and veils and promises—and she thought, This is what I want to do.

For the rest of the summer, she rode her bike to the library almost every day to draw and dream. During the school year she took art classes and every summer she returned to the library to copy the latest magazines. She majored in design in college and interned in New York, and gradually worked her way up to owning her own workshop.

It had been a long fierce climb, but she'd made it. She was successful, envied, happily married. But it was just an illusion. While she worked unceasingly to establish herself as one of New York's top designers, her loving husband had siphoned off their assets and disappeared.

The bank had taken everything else.

All she had left was her car and her reputation. The car was paid for, but her reputation wouldn't be worth a two-martini lunch once the news got out that M Atelier had gone belly up.

Margaux felt her chin quiver. Not now. She had one

more thing to do before she broke down and howled at the moon.

She slipped the business card out of her pocket and picked up her portfolio. She stepped into her secretary's office. "Guess we're the last two."

Yolanda looked up from a soggy Kleenex. Margaux thrust the business card toward her. "Liz Chang at DKNY has been threatening to steal you for years. Here's her number. Call her."

Yolanda took the card. "She'd take you, too."

Margaux shook her head. "Don't worry about me. I'll be fine." She'd thought about hiring herself out again. But the thought stuck in her gut. She couldn't do it. It was too humiliating. And she wouldn't give her competition the sastisfaction of seeing her grovel. Not yet, anyway.

"Good luck." Margaux turned to leave and came face-to-face with the most recent photo of herself. An awards dinner at the Plaza. Tall, sleek, her impossibly curly auburn hair gelled, sprayed, and pulled back into a classic French twist that an earthquake wouldn't ruffle. Her black evening gown, one of her own designs, had stopped conversation when she'd entered the room. She was holding a glass of Taittinger's champagne and smiling. At the top of her game.

And now the game was over.

She walked across the long expanse of wooden floor to the elevator, her heels tapping in the deserted room. She stepped inside and closed the grate; listened to the rhythmic creak as the ancient elevator descended to the ground floor one last time, stood as it clanked at the bottom, then pushed open the door to the street.

The air was thick with car fumes and the noise of living. Handcarts filled with goods rattled up the sidewalk. Garbage bags lined the curb. Men late for appointments shouldered past slower pedestrians. An old woman stuck her mittened hand out at Margaux. "Help an old lady?"

Margaux couldn't even help herself. She no longer belonged here, had no place here, no business, no apartment, no income.

There was only one place she could go.

NICK PRESCOTT GLANCED up as the blip appeared on his radar. Resignedly, he tossed his History of the Ostrogoths in Italy onto the passenger seat beside him. He should be sitting in his office correcting final exams, not hiding in the trees waiting to ticket some unsuspecting speeder.

Nick flipped on the siren, pulled the cruiser onto the tarmac, and took off after a bright blue sports coupe going at least sixty. The tourist season hadn't even begun, and already the summer people were breaking the law.

The car slowed and pulled to the sandy shoulder of the road. Nick followed and stopped several yards behind it. He noted the make, model, and license plate—New York—of course. Connecticut was their weekend retreat of choice.

As he got out of the cruiser, he slipped on his sunglasses and unsnapped his holster. He'd been out of the army for ten years, and until six months ago, he never thought he'd ever use a firearm again.

A woman sat behind the wheel, the window was open,

her hair was windblown. Auburn, deep, rich, like burnished mahogany. A color that as a boy stopped him in his tracks. It stopped him now, even while his rational mind told him it couldn't be her.

He took a breath and stepped up to the car. "Ma'am."

She looked up at him with wide, serious blue eyes. Eyes the color of a sunlit sea.

He'd know her anywhere in spite of the years that had passed. Felt the same jolt of connection he'd felt twenty years before. It hadn't changed, hadn't softened or diminished. And was still just as one-sided as it had always been. She had no idea who he was. "Do you know how fast you were going?"

"Fifty-five?"

"Sixty."

"But . . . that's only five over the speed limit."

"It was—a mile back. But you've entered Crescent Cove and it's thirty here."

A worried expression flitted across her face. "I didn't see the sign."

"Driver's license."

She riffled through an expensive-looking handbag and came up with an even more expensive-looking wallet.

"Take it out, please."

She jimmied the license out of the plastic sheath and handed it to him. Her fingers trembled a little.

"Margaux Sullivan."

She jumped as if the sound of her own name was a surprise. He frowned at the license, mainly to keep from staring at her.

She clutched the edge of the window. Her nail polish was chipped. She definitely had been biting her nails. The cuticles, too. Not something you'd expect from a hotshot New York fashion designer. And though she had turned into a beautiful woman, there were dark circles under her eyes and she looked drawn, not just model-thin. It made her eyes larger, vulnerable.

If this is what the big city did to you, she could have it. He studied her license. "New York City."

"Yes."

"Around here, Ms. Sullivan, we stick to the speed limit."

"I do, too," she assured him. "I just didn't realize I had entered the town limits."

"Uh-huh. Registration."

She fished in the glove compartment and handed it to him.

He took a look, then handed it back and pulled out a citation pad from his back pocket. It was his job after all.

"Officer," she pleaded.

"Chief of police."

"What? What happened to Herb Green?"

"Retired."

He didn't want to give her a ticket. Not with the way she was biting on her bottom lip. His heart was pounding and the sun beating down on his neck felt like a third-degree burn. He wanted to take her hand and tell her that whatever was making her look so unhappy would go away. He would make it go away. But he didn't. She'd been speeding, not five miles over, but twenty-five over. Ignorance was no excuse.

He handed her the ticket. "Drive carefully."

When she eased the Toyota onto the road, he pulled out behind her. He stayed behind her all the way into town, down Main Street to the other side of town where it joined Shore Road. He followed her until she turned through the chain-link gate of Little Crescent Beach. She was on her way home, and that open gate might as well have slammed shut behind her.

He jammed on the accelerator and sped away. For a few minutes he'd been young again. Just a townie boy with an ordinary dream. Not an ordinary man with no dreams left.

MARGAUX GRIPPED THE steering wheel in an effort to keep from shaking. She didn't have the money to pay for a speeding ticket. She barely had enough to pay for gas. When she'd slid her card into the gas pump on the way up, she prayed that it wouldn't be denied.

She drove slowly down Salt Marsh Lane, staring straight ahead, not even glancing at the summer house her best friend Bri's family owned, or at the cottage Grace's family rented each summer. She blinked away tears so close to the surface they hurt, but she resisted the urge to speed toward sanctuary. Most of the cottages were still boarded over from the winter, but small towns had a way of noticing things. It would be hard enough facing everyone without having to explain why she'd come running back or why the police had followed her home.

When the lane reached the beach, it curved to the right.

Three houses later, Margaux turned left into the parking niche at the back of the Sullivan beach house.

She took her suitcase and a bag of groceries out of the trunk and dumped them at the back door. She didn't go inside but took the path between the houses to the beach, scuffing through the sand, her head bowed, letting her shoes fill up with the heavy grains and her hair blow wild in the salt air.

She knew exactly when to look up. The perfect moment for that first full view. The blues of the water reaching up to the sky. The white sand stretching to each side in a graceful curve, like a smile.

When she was a kid, she would throw her arms open to the sea, let it take her troubles away. No matter how sad or angry or hurt she'd been, the waves could wash the feeling away. Could make her problems seem not so bad.

Margaux was older and wiser now and knew the waves couldn't fix what was wrong in her life, but at least they might give her some temporary respite.

There was one family on the beach, clustered beneath a bright umbrella near the empty lifeguard station. Farther along, two figures crawled over the rock jetty looking for crabs.

She sat down on the porch steps, closed her eyes, and lifted her face to the sun. Spots danced on her eyelids, the waves murmured in her ears. She concentrated on breathing and gradually her body began to relax. The knots in her shoulders eased. Her stomach gave up its churning, and she drifted back to a place where each day was a promise, and joy was just waking up to the cries of the gulls.

She lost track of time, maybe she dozed. When she opened her eyes again, the sky had turned from blue to mauve and the sun sat like a fiery fat beach ball on the horizon. The crabbers were gone. The family gathered up towels and their cooler and trudged up the beach toward home.

A solitary gull strutted near the water's edge, his bill jackhammering the sand in search of food. A wave rolled in; he swooped into the sky and was swallowed by the dusk.

Margaux was alone.

Lights began to come on in the condominium complex two coves away where her mother lived. Was Jude sitting on her balcony watching the sunset? Could she see Margaux? And what would she think if she did?

Would her failure become one of those moments printed indelibly on the memory, linked forever with these steps, this porch. Posing for pictures in her white First Communion dress. Chasing sand crabs that Danny had dumped on Jude's lap to proudly show off his catch. Louis's proposal. Dad, Jude, and her sitting together the Sunday after Danny died. And sitting with her mother, years later, when Henry Sullivan followed his son.

From deep inside the house the telephone rang. Resolutely, Margaux stood and climbed the steps to the porch. A rectangle of wood hung from a nail beneath the porch light; its black letters spelled out The Sullivans. She lifted the sign. Paint flakes drifted to the floor; a spider, disturbed from sleep, scuttled beneath the cedar shakes. She extracted the house key and let the sign fall back into place.

The lock was stiff and she had to lean against the door to

open it. But when she stepped over the threshold, she stopped, suddenly terrified. What had she been thinking? How could she come back like this—jobless, husbandless, childless. How could she face Jude with her boundless compassion and unfailing optimism.

The phone continued to ring. She groped her way across the dark foyer and picked up the receiver.

"You're there," said Jude's familiar voice.

"I'm here."

"I saw you from my terrace. Why didn't you let me know you were coming? I would have aired the house."

"It was a spur-of-the-moment thing."

"Are you free for dinner?"

"Sure, but let's eat here."

"Deke's? I can pick up food and be there in an hour."

"Deke's would be great." Margaux replaced the receiver and closed her eyes. She didn't think clam rolls were exactly what she needed to salvage her life. But maybe her mother could help.

JUDE SLID THE glass doors shut and called Deke's Clam Shack.

"Holy cow," said Deke O'Halloran. "The only reason you'd be eating fried is if Mags was home."

"She's home," Jude said, trying to keep the worry out of her voice. It wasn't like Margaux to show up unannounced. It wasn't like her to show up at all. She hadn't been back in years.

"Twenty minutes," Deke said. "I'll put on a fresh batch."

Jude hung up. When she'd seen the figure sitting on the front steps of the beach house and recognized her daughter, her heart leapt to her throat. Something it hadn't done in a long while.

Margaux never told her the real reason she and Louis had stopped coming to the shore, though Jude suspected it had nothing to do with how busy she was. She'd just about given up hope of them coming again, but she kept the house clean anyway—just in case. Jude had been disappointed but not surprised when Margaux called to say she'd filed for divorce. She didn't say why, only that things weren't working and that she could handle it.

Jude was proud of Margaux's strength. She had always known what she wanted, worked hard to get there. But that strength had become brittle in the last few years and Jude was worried. Strength ebbed and flowed, but brittle would break.

Well, whatever it was, they would see it through together. She glanced at the clock. Time to go. And on her way, she'd stop by the church to light a candle to the saints; her daughter had come home.

Margaux sat at the kitchen table, running her bare toes across the old linoleum floor, scratched from years of sandy feet. She was tired, she wanted to be alone, to stay in this cozy old kitchen while its dark maple cabinets and wallpaper of watering cans and ivy created a cocoon of safety around her.

But she knew that was impossible and when she heard

the familiar beep-beep of Jude's Citroën as it pulled into the drive, she dragged herself from the chair and went to meet her.

Jude bustled through the door, carrying a greasy paper bag and a six-pack of Budweiser. She was trim and fit, a few inches shorter than Margaux with the same auburn red hair. She was sixty-two but she had a new hairstyle that made her look years younger. She put down her parcels and opened her arms. Margaux walked into a hug. Her mother's cologne mingled with the smell of fresh fried clams, and the aroma was enough to make her cry.

Jude gave her a squeeze. "Let's eat. Deke'll kill me if the clams get cold. He put on a fresh batch just for you."

Margaux pulled away. "You told him I was here?"

"Well, of course." Jude frowned. "Shouldn't I—"

"You have a new hairdo. It looks great."

"Whole town does. Even Dottie, if you can believe that. New girl. From Brooklyn of all places. Bought the old Cut 'n Curl across from the marina. And a sheer genius." She smiled at her own joke. "By the way, Dottie said she better see you at the diner first thing tomorrow morning."

"Dottie knows, too?" She'd hoped to hibernate for a while, but now that was impossible. Dottie's Diner was the local gossip exchange.

Jude opened the bag and placed two foil-wrapped paper cartons on the table. "I was supposed to meet her for girls' night. Had to call to tell her I wasn't coming." She flipped the tab of one can, then stopped and peered at Margaux. "Is there a reason you don't want people to know you're here?"

"No." Margaux sat down at the table.

Jude sat down, too, but she didn't take her eyes off Margaux. "Is something wrong?"

Margaux shook her head, nodded.

Jude handed her a napkin. "Eat. Then we'll talk. There's nothing in this world that can't be fixed."

Margaux picked up her clam roll. It was so stuffed with succulent clams that a handful fell out when she bit into the roll.

They ate in silence. When Margaux had scooped up the last clam bit, Jude put down her beer. "Now tell me what's happened."

Margaux took a breath but the words stuck in her throat. She took another breath. "In a nutshell. While I was climbing the ladder of haute couture, becoming famous and building a nest egg so we could start a family, Louis stole everything. Savings, investments, everything, then dropped out of sight. I've lost the apartment, my business—"

"What? No. This can't be."

"He—" Margaux's voice cracked; a tear escaped and rolled down her cheek. She sucked in air. "They repossessed everything. Patterns, machines, fabric, even the drafting paper. I only had enough credit left to pay my staff.

"And my designs. They shoved them into cardboard boxes and took them away. What could the bank possibly want with them?"

She felt a hand on her shoulder and she turned into her mother and held on for dear life. "I've lost everything. How could Louis do this?"

And how could she have been so stupid not to notice before it was too late?

"Why didn't you call me? I could have transferred funds, sold the condo."

"It was over before I knew what was happening. Besides, I couldn't ask you to bail me out. It wouldn't have done any good. We're talking about a couple million."

Jude pulled away abruptly. "I'll call a lawyer I know. We'll stop this."

"I have a lawyer. She had the court freeze whatever assets were left. There wasn't much. She has a forensic accountant trying to trace the money, but they may never find it, if he still has it."

Margaux groped for a napkin. "You hear about this kind of thing all the time and you think, That could never happen to me. I'd never be so stupid. And look." She held out her hands. "Everything I dreamed of, worked for. Gone. I was on the brink of making it big, and now, zip, nada, nothing." The thin control she'd been holding on to for the last few weeks broke and she cried, sobbing in big gulps and not caring. "I would have given him half—money, property— more than half. I only wanted one thing and he took that, too."

Jude pushed a wild strand of hair from Margaux's cheek. "What?"

"My future."

"Oh, Margaux. It only seems that way now. You were right to come home."

Margaux sniffed. "Where else could I go?" She hated herself for sounding so needy, so incapable, but she'd used up every reservoir of strength just getting through the last two months.

"No place else in the world. You've got family and friends and a home. You'll create more designs, make more money, and someday you'll meet someone to love and have a family with."

"Mom, I'm thirty-four."

"Thirty-four is nothing. Women have children into their forties these days."

"There won't be anyone else."

"Of course there will be. It's early days yet."

"There wasn't for you."

"No." Jude smiled. "You're exhausted. Things will look better when you've rested. Why don't you come stay at the condo with me tonight?"

"Thanks, but—" Margaux shook her head.

"Or . . . I could stay here."

"No. I just need to sleep. You go on home. I'll be fine."

"Are you sure?"

"I'll be fine. I promise."

Jude gathered up their trash. "Okay, but call me if you change your mind. Doesn't matter what time. I mean it."

"I will." Margaux walked her to the car.

Jude kissed her good night. "Dottie's for waffles. I'll pick you up at nine."

"Mom, I can't."

"Sure you can. You don't want to hurt Dottie's feelings and you need to eat."

Margaux gave in. It took more than she had to resist. By tomorrow she'd be able to hold herself together. For a while anyway.

Jude beeped as she rounded the curve and Margaux went inside. She was numb with shock, with pain, with sheer exhaustion, but she knew she wouldn't be able to sleep. It seemed like she hadn't slept in years, and the stairs to her bedroom seemed to stretch forever.

She walked through the parlor and out the front door.

She hesitated at the bottom of the porch steps. The beach was dark, the sand eerily illuminated by the sliver of moon. She took a step and the sand shifted beneath her feet. Another step, another shift. Another . . . and another until the sand turned wet and hard. Another and another until she stood ankle deep in the cold water of the Sound.

She looked into the darkness, opened her arms, and gave in to the pull of the tide, strong, relentless, its siren call singing her home.

And read an exclusive excerpt from
Shelley Noble's latest

Stargazey Point

Chapter One

· · · · · · · · ·

HATE. HOW MANY times a day did that word come up in conversation? I hate these shoes with this outfit. I hate Jell-O with fruit. People laugh and say I hate it when that happens. Hate could be a joke. Or an all-consuming fire that singed your spirit before eating your soul.

Abbie Sinclair had seen it in all its forms, okay maybe not all, and for that she was thankful, but in too many forms to process, to turn a cold eye, to keep plugging away in spite of it all.

A sad commentary on someone who had just turned thirty. Somehow, Abbie thought that the big three-oh would set her free, leave the crushed, dispirited twenties behind. But as the therapist told her during her first session, she wouldn't be able to go forward until she came to terms with her past. She didn't go back—to the therapist or the past.

So here she was five thousand feet above Indiana, Kentucky, or some other state, on her way from Chicago to South Carolina, thinking about hate instead of worrying about what to have for dessert instead of Jell-O or what shoes *would* go with this outfit.

Abbie knew she had to jettison her hate or it would destroy her. But no matter how many times she'd written the word, torn the paper into little strips, shredded it, burned it, ran water over it until it disintegrated, stepped on it. No matter how many times she'd symbolically thrown it away, forced it out of her heart, there seemed to be just a little left, and it would grow back, like pus in an infected wound.

Pus? Really? Had she really just made that analogy? Abbie pressed her fingers to her temples. The absolute lowest. Purple prose. Bad writing and ineffective emotion, something her mentor and lover insisted had no place in cutting-edge documentaries. Something her post-flower-child mother insisted had no place anywhere in life. And something that her best friend, Celeste, said was just plain tacky.

Besides, it didn't come close to what she really felt.

Abbie had been full of fire when she started out. She'd planned to expose the evils of the world, do her part in righting injustice, make people understand and change. The Sinclairs' youngest daughter would finally join the ranks of her do-gooding family. Instead, that fire had turned inward and was destroying her. How arrogant and naïve she had been. How easily she'd lost hope.

"Don't be so hard on yourself," Celeste said when Abbie showed up at her apartment with one jungle-rotted duffel bag and a bucketful of tears. "You can probably get your old job back. Want me to ask?"

Abbie just wanted to sleep, except with sleep came dreams peopled by the dead, asking why, why, why of the living.

They decided what she needed was a change of scene. At least that's what Celeste decided. Somewhere comfortable with people who were kind. Celeste knew just the place. With her relatives in a South Carolina beach town named Stargazey Point.

"You'll like it there," Celeste said. "And you'll love Aunt Marnie and Millie and Uncle Beau. They're really my great- or maybe it's my great-great- . . . but they're sweethearts and they'd love to have you."

It did sound good; quiet, peaceful, sun and surf. "I'll go," Abbie said.

She was a basket case. She needed therapy. She went on vacation instead.

Celeste drove her to O'Hare. "You'll have to take a cab from the airport. I don't think they drive anymore. It'll take about forty minutes if there's no traffic and cost about sixty dollars. Here." She thrust a handful of bills at Abbie, then tried to take her coat. "You won't need it there."

Abbie refused the money and clung to her coat. She didn't need it. That burning emotion she couldn't kill was enough to keep her warm on the coldest day.

There was a mini bottle of unopened chardonnay on the tray table before her. She was still clutching her coat.

She wasn't ordinarily a slow learner. And she usually

didn't run. That had changed in a heartbeat. And that's when the hate rushed in.

She hated the company whose arrogance had washed away an entire schoolroom of children and the boy and his donkey, hated the security people who had smashed their cameras, hated those who stood by and watched or ran in terror, who dragged her away when she was only trying to save someone, anyone. Those who arrested Werner and threw him in a jail where he met with an "unfortunate accident."

For that she hated them most of all. Selfish, but there it was. They had killed Werner on top of everything else.

And there was not a damn thing she could do about it. There was no footage, no Werner, she'd barely escaped before they confiscated her visa. Others weren't so lucky.

The tears started, she forced them back. How could she allow herself tears when everyone else had suffered more?

"SHE SHOULD BE here any minute now, sister, and you haven't gotten out the tea service. Do you think it's goin' to polish itself? And look how you're dressed."

Marnie Crispin glanced down at her dungarees and the old white T-shirt that Beau had put out for the veterans' box, then looked at her younger sister and sighed. Millie was dressed in a floral print shirtwaist that had to be twenty years old, but was pressed like it had just come off the rack at Belks Department Store.

"I know how I'm dressed, the garden doesn't weed itself.

I'm planning to change. And I'm not getting out the tea service."

"But, sister."

"You don't want to scare the girl away, do you?"

"No," said Millie, patting at the white wisps of hair that framed her thin face. "But she's come all the way from Chicago, poor thing. And I want everything to be just perfect for her. Beau, you're dropping shavings all over my carpet."

Their younger brother, who would turn seventy-nine in two months, was sitting in his favorite chintz-covered chair, the ubiquitous block of wood and his pocketknife in hand. He looked down at his feet and the curls of wood littered there.

"Oh." He attempted to push them under the chair with the side of his boot.

"How many times have I told you not to drop shavings on my carpet?"

Beau rocked forward and pushed himself to his feet.

"Where do you think you're going?"

Beau looked down at the carving in his hand, back at Millie. "Going to watch out for that taxicab from the front porch."

Millie pursed her lips, but there was no rancor in it. Beau was Beau and they loved him. "Just you mind you don't drop shavings all over my porch."

Beau shuffled out of the room.

"And tuck that shirttail in," Millie called after him.

CABOT MONTGOMERY HEARD the car go by. They didn't get much sightseeing this time of year, a few fishermen, an occasional antiquer, a handful of diehard sun worshipers, though most of them preferred the more upscale hotels of Myrtle Beach.

There were a few year-round residents and hearing a car wasn't all that unusual. In the year he'd lived here he'd come to recognize the characteristic sound of just about every car, truck, and motorcycle in the area. And he didn't recognize the one that had just passed. Which could only mean one thing.

Wiping his hands on a well-used chamois, he climbed over the engine housing and looked out between the broken lattice of the window. Whoever it was had come and gone.

He tossed the chamois on his worktable, lifted his keys off the peg by the door, and stopped to look around as he did at the end of every workday. For a full minute he just stood and breathed in the faint odor of machine oil, mildew, and childhood memories.

He tried to imagine the time when he'd stop for the day, look up and see all the work he'd put into the old derelict building gleaming back at him; the colored lights refracting off the restored mirrors bursting into fractured reds, blues, and yellows, while music swirled around his head and the smell of fresh sawdust curled in his nostrils.

So far he only saw a dark almost empty room, locked away from the world by a sagging plywood door. Right now he only saw how much more there was to do. But never once since he'd returned had he ever looked over the space and thought, What the hell have I done?

Cabot padlocked the door then crossed the street to Hadley's, the local grocery store, bait shop, and gas station. He jogged up the wooden steps to the porch and was just pulling a Coke out of the old metal ice chest when Silas Cook came out the door, a string bag of crabs slung over his shoulder. He dropped the bag into a bucket of water and sat down on the steps. Cab sat down beside him and took a long swig off the bottle of Coke.

"You see that taxicab drive through town a while back?" Silas asked.

"I heard it. Did you?"

"Sure did. Me and Hadley came right out here on the porch and watched it drive by."

"See the passenger?"

"A girl come all the way from Chicag-ah."

Cabot nodded. Like Chicago was the end of the earth.

"You goin' on over there?" asked Silas, nodding down the street toward the old Crispin House.

"After I get cleaned up. I finagled myself an invitation to dinner."

"Well, you in luck there, 'cause I just dropped off a dozen of the finest lady blue claws you'll see this season. Told Ervina she oughta just drop 'em in de pot, but Miz Millie, she want crab bisque. So she gonna make crab bisque."

Cabot leaned back and rested his elbows on the top step. "Fine dining and a chance to get a good, close look at the Crispins' guest. Find out just what she's up to."

"What do you think she's up to? She's a friend of their niece's, like they said, come on vacation."

"Maybe. But what do we know about their niece? They haven't seen her in years. Maybe she sees a gold mine waiting to be exploited."

Silas pushed to his feet and looked down at Cab. "Go on, Mr. Cab. You don't trust much of nobody, do you?"

Cabot was taken aback. "Why do you say that? I trust you, and Hadley, and Beau, and—"

"I mean other people."

"Sure I do."

"You more protective of this town than folks who've lived here all their lives, and their daddies and granddaddies, too."

"You gotta protect what's yours, you should know that, Silas."

"Yessuh, I know it. And I learnt it the hard way. I just don't get why you knows it. Well, I'd best be getting these gals in my own pot." Silas started down the steps; when he got to the bottom, he turned back to Cabot. "You tell Mr. Beau, I'm going out fishin' tomorrah if he wanna come."

"I will." Cabot gave the older man a quick salute and finished his Coke while he watched Silas walk down the street. Then he went inside to pay for his drink.

"One Co-cola," Hadley said, punching the keys of an ancient cash register. "You see Silas outside?"

"Yeah," Cab said. "I'm getting crab bisque at the Crispins' tonight."

"Did he also tell you we seen their visitor?"

"Yep."

"She was a pretty thing as far as I could see. Pale as a ghost, though, even her hair, kinda whitelike. She looked out of the window just as she passed by and I swear it was like she looked right into me. It was kinda spooky."

"Spooky or speculative? Like someone planning to cheat the Crispins out of their house and land?"

"Don't know about that. Silas says they're expecting her. Friend of their great-niece's or some such."

"Maybe," Cabot agreed. "I'll keep an eye on her."

"Know you will, son. Know you will."

Cabot walked home, thinking about the Crispins and his uncle Ned, who was the reason he was here. Or at least the reason that brought him to Stargazey Point this last time. Ned had died and left Cabot everything.

He'd hardly seen his uncle since he graduated from high school over fifteen years ago. But before that he'd spent every summer with Ned, working long hours at the now defunct boardwalk.

He'd driven from Atlanta to settle Ned's estate. It wasn't much, the old octagonal building, a small tin-roofed cottage in the back side of town. And the contents of a shed situated inland and watched over by an ancient Gullah man named Abraham.

That discovery had sealed his fate. The memories of the magical summers he'd spent with Ned broke through the high-pressured, high-tech world he inhabited, and he knew he had to recapture that magic. He gave up his "promising" career as an industrial architect for an uncertain future. Traded his minimalist designed, state of the art apartment for a rotten porch, broken windows, and peeling paint.

According to his Atlanta colleagues, he'd lost his mind.

When he asked his fiancée Bailey to move to Stargazey Point with him, she accused him of playing Peter Pan. Just before she threw her two karat engagement ring at his head.

Peter Pan or crazy, he didn't care. He was working longer hours than he had in Atlanta, but he fell into bed each night and slept like a baby until sunrise. Woke up each morning with a clear conscience and he felt alive.

Things had changed in the years since he'd been here. People had been hit hard. Houses sat empty, where their owners had given up and sold out or just moved on. All around them real estate was being gobbled up by investors.

Hadley was right; he didn't trust people. Especially ones who came with big ideas on how to improve their little, mostly forgotten town—starting with selling all your property to them. He knew those people, hell, he'd been one of those people.

And now suddenly, out of the blue, a friend of the niece shows up, which was a stretch considering they hadn't seen their great-niece in years. He'd tried to convince the Crispins not to let her stay in the house. They knew nothing about her; she might have ulterior motives and he'd be damned if he'd let those three be taken advantage of. They were proud, slightly dotty, and close to penniless. Vulnerable to any scam.

Abbie Sinclair. Just the name sounded like pencil skirts and four-inch heels. A calfskin briefcase attached to a slender hand with perfectly manicured fingernails, talons just waiting to snatch away their home and way of life.

ABBIE SHOULD HAVE seen it coming once the taxi entered the tunnel of antebellum oak trees. One second she'd been looking at the ocean, the next the sun disappeared and they bounced along uneven ground beneath an archway of trees. The temperature dropped several degrees, and her eyes strained against the sudden darkness to see ahead. Another minute and they were spit out into the sunshine again.

And there was Crispin House.

It was more than a house, more like a southern plantation. Not the kind with big white columns, but three-storied white wood and stucco, with wraparound porches on the upper two floors. The first floor was supported by a series of stone arches that made Abbie think of a monastery with dark robed monks going about their daily chores in the shadows. Italianate, if she remembered her architectural styles correctly.

The taxi stopped at the steps that led up to the front door. For a long minute she just sat in the backseat of the cab and stared.

"Whooo," the driver whistled. "Somebody shore needs to give that lady a coat of paint."

He was right. The house had been sorely neglected. She just hoped the inside was in better shape.

She could see spots of peeling paint and a few unpainted balusters where someone had repaired the porch rail. There was a patch of uneven grass and one giant solitary oak that spread its branches over the wide front steps, casting the porch in shadow.

This was crazy. Celeste had merely said her relatives would love to have her stay with them, they had plenty of room. She hadn't said that they could have housed a large portion of the Confederate Army. Well, she'd stay one night, and if things didn't work out, she'd seen an inn in the little town they'd just driven through. It at least had a coat of paint.

She paid the driver, added a generous tip since it seemed that he wouldn't have any return fares, and prepared to meet the Crispin family.

There was movement on the porch, and Abbie realized that a man had been sitting on the rail watching her. He stood, fumbled in his pockets, brushed his palms together and started down the stairs, lean and lanky and moving slow, his knees sticking out to the side with each downward step.

Abbie reached for the car door handle, but the door opened and a face appeared in the opening. His skin was crinkled and deeply lined from the sun. A shock of thick white hair had escaped from his carefully groomed part and stuck up above his forehead. Bright blue eyes twinkled beneath bushy white eyebrows and managed to appear both fun-loving and wise at the same time. Abbie suspected he'd been quite handsome as a young man. He still was.

"Miz Sinclair?"

"Yes," Abbie said, though it took her a second to recognize her own name. In its slow delivery, it sounded more like "Sinclayuh." It was soft and melodious, like a song, and she relaxed just a little. "You must be Mr. Crispin."

"Yes'm, that's me. But folks 'round here all call me Beau." He held out a large bony hand, the veins thick as ropes across the back, then he snatched it back, rubbed it vigorously on his pants leg and presented it again.

Abbie smiled up at Beauregard Crispin, took his proffered hand and got out of the car.

The driver carried her two bags up to the porch. "Ya'll have a nice stay," he said, then nodded to Mr. Crispin, got back in the taxi, and drove away.

Abbie felt a moment of panic. She had a feeling there might not be another taxi for miles.

"After you."

She hesitated, just looking at Beau's outstretched hand, then she forced a smile and began to climb the wide wooden steps. She'd just reached the porch when the screen door opened and two women stepped out of the rectangle of darkness. They had to be Millie and Marnie. The Crispin sisters.

"*Here's the thing about my relatives,*" Celeste told her. "*They're sweet as pie, but they're old fashioned. I mean really old fashioned, like pre–Civil War old fashioned.*"

Abbie had laughed; well, her version of a laugh these days. "*I get it, they're old fashioned. No four letter words, no politics, no religion. Not to worry, I have better sense than to talk politics to people who lost the wahr.*"

"*The what?*"

"*The war. That was my attempt at a southern accent. No good?*"

Celeste shook her head. "*Not by a long shot.*" She dropped into a speech pattern that she'd nearly erased through much practice and four years of studying communications. "*The wahuh. Two syllables and soft. It's South Carolina, not Texas. We're refined. We've got Charleston.*"

Abbie impulsively grabbed Celeste's hand. *"Don't you want to go with me?"*

"I'd love to but I can't get away from the station."

"When was the last time you had a vacation?"

"Can't remember. You know the media. Out of sight, out of— Go have a good time. Let them pamper you. They're experts."

Now, Abbie suddenly got it. She would have recognized them in a crowd. Millie, the younger sister, prim, petite, neatly dressed and hair coiffed in a tidy little bun at the nape of her neck. And Marnie, taller, raw-boned, dressed in a pair of dungarees and a tattered man's T-shirt smeared with dirt. Her white hair was thick and wild with curls. According to Celeste, Marnie was the only one who had left the fold, only to return fifty years later, the intervening years unspoken of, what she had done or where she had been a mystery.

"Us kids used to make up stories about her. Once we were convinced she was a spy for the CIA, then we decided she traveled to Paris and became the mistress of a tortured painter and posed nude for him. We were very precocious.

"She came for a visit once, but we weren't allowed to see her. She only stayed two days, and I heard Mama tell Daddy that she was drinking buttermilk the whole time she was there, 'cause it was the only thing she missed. And Daddy said it was because it covered the smell of the scotch she poured into it."

"They're teetotalers."

"Not at all. Aunt Millie has a sherry every afternoon."

"My de-ah," Millie Crispin said, coming forward and holding out both hands. "Welcome to Crispin House. We're so glad to have you. Beau, get Abbie's luggage and bring it inside."

"Please, I can—" But that was as far as she got before she was swept across the threshold by the deceptively fragile-looking Millie.

"Now you just come inside and leave everything to Beau."

Abbie didn't want to think of Beau struggling with her suitcases, but she saw Marnie slip past them to give her brother a hand, just before Millie guided her through a wide oak door and into a high-ceiling foyer.

"I thought you might like to see your room first and get settled in," Millie said in her soft drawl.

"Thank you." Abbie followed her up a curved staircase to the second floor, matching her steps to Millie's slower ones.

At the top of the stairs, a landing overlooked the foyer. A portrait of a man in uniform hung above a side table and a large Chinese vase. Three hallways led to the rest of the house.

Millie started down the center hall. "We've put you in the back guest suite. Celeste and her mama and daddy used to stay there when they visited." Millie sighed. "There's a lovely view." She chattered on while Abbie followed a footstep behind her and tried to decipher the pattern of the faded oriental runner.

They came to the end of the hall and Millie opened a door. "Heayuh we are. I hope you like everything." They stepped inside to a large darkened room. A row of wooden shutters blocked the light from the windows and a set of French doors that hopefully led to a balcony. Millie hurried over to the windows and opened the shutters. Slices of sunlight poured in, revealing an elegant but faded love seat and several chairs.

"Over here is your bedroom," Millie said, guiding Abbie through another door to another room, this one fitted out with a high four-poster bed with the same shuttered door and windows. Millie bustled about the room opening the shutters and pointing out amenities. "The bath's through there . . ."

Millie's words buzzed about Abbie's ears. She appreciated Millie's desire to be welcoming, but she wanted—needed—solitude, anonymity, not someone hovering solicitously over her every second. Coming here had been a big mistake.

"If you need anything, anything at all, you just pull that bellpull and Ervina will come see to you."

Ervina? Was there another sister Celeste hadn't told her about?

"You just make yourself at home. We generally have dinner at six, but come down anytime you like."

Abbie followed her back into the sitting room and to the door. "Now you have a rest and then we'll have a nice visit." Millie finally stepped into the hallway.

Abbie shut the door on Millie's smile and leaned against it.

There was a tap behind her that made Abbie jump away from the door. *Be patient*, she told herself. *She's trying to be nice.* She opened the door.

Marnie was there with her suitcases. Abbie opened the door wider and Marnie lugged them in. She was followed by an even older African-American woman carrying a tray.

"You shouldn't have carried my bags."

"No bother. We send the luggage up on a dumb waiter. Ervina, put that tray over on the Hepplewhite."

Ervina wasn't a sister. She was the servant. And she was ancient.

Ervina shuffled into the room, carrying a tray laden with cups, saucers and plates of food, that looked heavier than the woman who carried it. Abbie felt a swell of outrage and fought not to take the load from the woman.

Marnie walked through the room turning on several lamps. "We'll leave you alone. Millie insisted on the tray. Don't overeat because she's going to feed you again in a couple of hours. And don't worry that you'll be trapped in the house listening to two old broads talk your ear off. You just do however you want. Come, Ervina, let's leave the poor girl alone." Marnie headed for the door.

Ervina followed. She slanted a look at Abbie as she passed by, nodded slowly as if Abbie had just met her expectations, then shuffled through the door and shut it without a backwards look.

Bemused, Abbie turned off the lamps Marnie had just turned on. They had to be conserving electricity. Because from the little she'd seen of Crispin House, shabby genteel wasn't just a lifestyle, it was a necessity.

And then there was the elaborate tea tray, sterling silver, filled with cakes and little sandwiches with the crusts cut off, tea in a bone china pot, and a pitcher of lemonade.

"Celeste, I could brain you. What the hell have you gotten me into?"

Abbie took a cucumber sandwich and crossed to the

French doors. After fumbling one-handed with the handle, she popped the rest of the little sandwich in her mouth and used both hands to pull the doors open.

She stepped out to the wraparound porch where several white rocking chairs and wicker side tables were lined up facing the ocean. The air was tangy with salt, and she breathed deeply before crossing to the rail.

Below her a wide lawn slid into white dunes that dipped and billowed before the old mansion like a crinoline. Delicate tufts of greenery embroidered the way to the beach, wide and white and ending in a point that stretched like a guiding finger to the horizon.

And beyond that, water and sky. She'd come to the edge of the world. Not a violent wave-crashing, jagged-rock edge that you'd expect, but the southern genteel version with fat lazy waves rolling in, tumbling one over the other before spilling into white foam on the sand.

Abbie filled her lungs with the spicy, clean air and slowly let it out. Part of her tension oozed away. She was tempted just to stay right there looking at the ocean forever, but they were expecting her for dinner.

She went inside to unpack. Her coat was lying across the chenille bedspread.

Her cell phone rang. She turned her back on the coat and checked caller ID.

"Perfect timing," she said, answering it.

"Did you just arrive?" Celeste asked.

"A few minutes ago. This place is incredible, kind of southern gothic."

"Ugh. Is it in really bad shape? I've been meaning to get back but I never seem to find the time."

"The outside more than the interior, though it looks like someone has started repairs. But everything is very comfortable, the sisters are a hoot, and Beau . . . I adore him already."

"Which room did they give you?"

"One with peach paint that opens onto the veranda and a view of the ocean. Why didn't you tell me about the beach?"

"I did."

"Oh, well it's incredible. I haven't had a chance to go down yet, but I plan to spend tomorrow laying out. Thank you."

"No prob. Don't forget your sunscreen. It isn't hot yet, but the sun can burn. Especially with your skin."

"Thanks, Ma."

"Oh hell, I know you know more about sunburn than I do, considering the sun hardly ever creeps into my office." Celeste sighed. "I'm kind of envious."

"Then why don't you try to get away? It's really quite wonderful," Abbie said. And her stay here would be easier to handle with Celeste to deflect some of the attention.

"I wish. I told you it was just what you needed. You have to promise to soak up some rays for me."

"I will and you were right. Even if I had to fall apart to realize it."

"Don't think about that. You'll get back into it—when you're ready."

And nobody, not even Abbie, thought she would ever be ready. She knew she could never go back. Back had been torn away from her. Back was no longer an option.

"Hey listen, I have a very important question for you."

"Yes?"

Abbie could hear the wariness in her friend's voice. "Am I expected to dress for dinner?"

Celeste laughed. It was a sound that made Abbie feel homesick.

"Well, I haven't been there in years, but it is Sunday dinner."

"I take that to mean yes. But how dressed?"

"You know, just nice, a dress, not too short, maybe some pearls."

"Got it. I'd better get hopping. I don't want to be late. And Celeste. Thanks. I take it back, all that stupid stuff I said. You were right. This is just what I needed."

About the Author

· · · · · · · · ·

A former professional dancer and choreographer, SHELLEY NOBLE lives in New Jersey.